A Kiss of Silk

Barbara Cartland

A Kiss of Silk

THORNDIKE
CHIVERS

This Large Print edition is published by Thorndike Press®, Waterville, Maine USA and by BBC Audiobooks Ltd, Bath, England.

Published in 2006 in the U.S. by arrangement with Cartland Promotions.

Published in 2006 in the U.K. by arrangement with Cartland Promotions, c/o Rupert Crew Limited.

U.S. Hardcover   0-7862-8298-3 (Candlelight)
U.K. Hardcover   1-4056-3697-1 (Chivers Large Print)
U.K. Softcover   1-4056-3698-X (Camden Lage Print)

The text of this Large Print edition is unabridged.
Other aspects of the book may vary from the original edition.

Set in 16 pt. Plantin by Al Chase.

Printed in the United States on permanent paper.

British Library Cataloguing-in-Publication Data available

Library of Congress Cataloging-in-Publication Data

Cartland, Barbara, 1902–
  A kiss of silk / by Barbara Cartland.
    p. cm. — (Thorndike Press large print Candlelight)
  ISBN 0-7862-8298-3 (lg. print : hc : alk. paper)
  I. Title.   II. Thorndike Press large print Candlelight series.
PR6005.A765K55 2006
 823'.912—dc22   2005030216

A Kiss of Silk

Chapter One

"Come on, Fluff! We've got to hurry."
Varia spoke to the small white poodle which
was prancing about with so much excitement that it was difficult to fasten the lead
to his collar.

At last, however, she achieved it and then,
running down the narrow mews, she
reached the street and the traffic.

It took only a few minutes to cross
Kensington High Street and they were in
the Park; but they were minutes which Varia
watched nervously because any delay meant
that she would be late at the office.

This morning everything had gone
wrong.

She had overslept, the alarm clock had
not gone off, and these catastrophes were
followed by others, all making her feel that
she was racing against time.

Anyway, at last they were in the Park
and she was running, with Fluff bounding

and barking beside her.

There was a pale sunshine glinting over the trees and on the great beds of banked tulips which were almost breathtaking in their colourful beauty.

And there was a wind which whipped Varia's pale curls against her cheeks, bringing the colour into them and making her eyes shine as she called out in a panting voice:

"Not . . . so quick . . . Fluff!"

The poodle was pulling her almost faster than her feet could carry her. Then, suddenly, it happened.

A tall figure seemed to appear from nowhere. Varia tried to check herself, to pull Fluff to her, but he went one way and she another, and with a sudden exclamation of surprise the tall figure tripped over the lead.

There was a yelp of pain from Fluff before Varia let him go and he sped away across the grass, his lead trailing behind him, while she was left looking down at the figure of a man, sprawling on one knee, on the ground beside her.

"I am sorry!" she said. "I do apologise. I can't think how it happened. Are you hurt?"

A pair of twinkling dark eyes looked up into hers.

"Do not apologise, *Ma'm'selle*," a deep

voice with a faint foreign accent replied. "All is well; but I was, as you say, taken by surprise."

"But I am sorry about it," Varia said. "We were hurrying and Fluff — that's my dog — was pulling at his lead. I am afraid I wasn't looking where we were going."

The man got slowly to his feet, his trousers were dusty and there were some small spots of blood on his hand.

"Oh, you're hurt!" Varia cried. "We must get something for your hand. Perhaps there is a chemist nearby."

She looked round a little wildly as if she expected a chemist's shop to spring up in the middle of Hyde Park. The stranger only laughed.

"It is nothing," he said. "Please do not trouble yourself about it."

"And your trousers!" Varia said. "They are so dusty."

"Dust will brush off," he answered reassuringly.

He smiled down at her and she realised how tall he was and, for that matter, how good-looking. But his dark, sun-burned face with high, rather prominent cheekbones, deep-set, dark eyes and a square forehead all seemed somehow unimportant beside his smile.

In fact, there was no doubt about it, his smile was irresistible.

"I can only say again how sorry I am," Varia breathed.

"And dare I say that I am glad because it gives us an opportunity to introduce ourselves," the stranger said. "We can consider this an introduction, can't we? Even in England — where it is such an important preliminary to any conversation."

Varia laughed — she could not help it — and he went on:

"As Fluff — who seems to have made up his mind to present us — has disappeared, may I tell you that I am Pierre de Chalayat, at your service?"

"You are French?" Varia asked.

"Didn't you guess?" he replied. "I cannot believe that my English is so perfect that you thought me a fellow countryman."

"No, I didn't think that," she said honestly. "But your English is very good."

"That is because I love England and, of course, the English people," he answered with an almost imperceptible little bow that somehow turned it into a very delicate compliment.

"My name is Varia Milfield," Varia said. "And now, please, if you will accept my apologies again, I must go. I shall be late at the office. Please forgive me, and I hope your hand will be all right."

She turned as she spoke and began running as swiftly as she could down Rotten Row with Fluff reluctantly following her.

She reached the offices where she worked at one second to nine o'clock.

She was hot and breathless, but she had the satisfaction of knowing that it had not yet struck nine as she passed in through the imposing, porticoed front door in a street which opened just off Park Lane. She then hurried quickly down to the basement.

The caretaker's wife, with a handkerchief round her head and a bucket in her hand, was just coming out of one of the rooms.

"I began to think you were going to be late this morning, Miss Milfield," she smiled.

"So did I," Varia replied.

"Ted was all of a fret in case the little dog didn't come," the woman said.

"How is Ted?" Varia enquired.

"He 'ad a better night, thank God," the woman answered. "In fact, 'e seems to be picking up altogether. I can't 'elp thinking that it's that dog that's done the trick. It seems to give 'im something to look forward to."

"I'm so glad," Varia said. "But I mustn't

11

stop here talking, Mrs. Huggins, I shall get the sack!"

"There was only one thing I was going to say to you, Miss," Mrs. Huggins said hastily. "You wouldn't think of selling the dog, would you?"

"Oh, no! I'm afraid I couldn't," Varia said hastily. "Fluff isn't mine. He belongs to my mother and she's ill, very ill, and she loves Fluff. It's only that it gives me a chance of giving him a walk when I come here and a walk when I go back at lunch time that makes it easy for Ted to have him. I just couldn't ask my mother to part with him."

"I understands," Mrs. Huggins answered. "It was only just an idea seeing 'ow young Ted 'as taken such a fancy to the little dog. But don't worry your 'ead, Miss Milfield. You've been kind enough as it is. We'll think of somethin'."

"Yes, of course, we will," Varia said. "You think and I'll think and we'll find something to keep Ted happy. I must go now."

She sped up the stairs, through the hall, and taking the lift, pressed the button for the top floor. As she stepped out and opened the door of the big office, she saw at once that she was last to arrive.

There was quite a chorus of: "You're late again!"

"I know, I know," she said. "Everything has gone wrong this morning."

"Oh, don't worry," one of the girls said. "Old Cranky isn't here."

Varia let out a sigh of relief. She was terrified of Miss Crankshaft, the head secretary, who had served Blakewell & Co. for over thirty years and never forgot to let those under her know about it.

Varia slipped out of the office and went to the cloakroom at the end of the passage; and when she saw her reflection in the glass, she realised that it was about time she tidied herself.

Her fair hair, blown by the wind, seemed to be standing up on end. Yet as she looked in the mirror her eyes, deep violet in colour, seemed to be alight with all the sunshine she had left outside in the Park.

She combed her hair, tidied her dress, washed her hands, then, looking demure and she hoped efficient, she went back to the office.

"Is that better, Sarah?" she asked as she sat at her desk.

"Much better," Sarah replied. "What have you been up to?"

"I had to run to get here," Varia confessed. "I overslept and then I burned Mummy's breakfast, and I had to change her pillow-case and the electric kettle wouldn't work! Oh, just everything went wrong!"

"I know that sort of day," Sarah sympathised.

"Then I ran into the Park as I always do and Fluff tripped up a stranger; that delayed me too."

"That's a new way of getting to know someone!" Sarah remarked. "Was he nice?"

"He was a Frenchman," Varia said a little drily.

"You be careful," Sarah admonished her. "You can't trust Frenchmen. Was he an attractive one?"

"Very attractive," Varia said.

"Worse and worse!" Sarah exclaimed. "It was quite obvious that Fluff didn't trip him up, but he tripped Fluff."

"Oh, Sarah, you are absurd!" Varia smiled.

She set the paper in her typewriter and settled down to the copy work that had been given to her the day before.

But all the same, she could not help thinking of the Frenchman and how his dark eyes had looked down into hers. Pierre de Chalayat! It was a nice name, a name she wouldn't forget easily.

She wondered if he would remember hers.

"Day-dreaming I suppose, Miss Milfield!" a voice snapped.

She looked up. Miss Crankshaft was standing there, looking more formidable than usual.

"I'm sorry, Miss Crankshaft," Varia said hastily. "I . . . I was just puzzling over what I had to do."

"It's not the first time I've had to speak to you, Miss Milfield," Miss Crankshaft snorted. "And I don't suppose it will be the last. You waste more time than any other girl in this office. Come along now, if you please."

"Come along?" Varia questioned. "But where to?"

"Sir Edward wishes to see you."

"Sir Edward!" Varia gasped. "Whatever for?"

"That you will doubtless learn in due course," Miss Crankshaft replied impressively. "Sir Edward has asked to see you and he does not like to be kept waiting."

Varia got to her feet, feeling suddenly apprehensive. Was she to get the sack? She couldn't think of any reason why Sir Edward would wish to see her.

Her thoughts were racing, but automatically she followed Miss Crankshaft out through the office door and down the

15

stairs to the first floor.

Miss Crankshaft gave her a quick look as if to reassure herself she was neat and tidy, and then knocked on a door and opened it at the same time.

"Miss Milfield, Sir Edward," she said, and ushered Varia into a large, imposing-looking room which she had never entered before.

The walls were panelled and there were two large desks which seemed to take up an unconscionable amount of space. Seated at one of them was Sir Edward Blakewell; standing beside him was his son, Ian.

Varia knew Mr. Ian Blakewell well enough by sight. He came regularly every day to the office and was, she knew, about twenty-eight years of age, extremely clever and very unapproachable.

He was not like his father, she had heard the older clerks say. Sir Edward bawled you out all right, but he always had a cheery word for everyone and knew more about his staff than they knew about themselves.

But since Varia had been working for Blakewell & Co., Sir Edward had come to the office very seldom. He had been abroad all the winter and she had, in fact, during the four months of her employment, only seen him two or three times in the distance.

For a moment there was silence and both men — the older and the younger one — seemed to stare at Varia.

Then, almost explosively, Mr. Ian Blakewell said:

"It's impossible, Father! I tell you, it's quite impossible!"

"And I tell you it's the only thing we can do," Sir Edward replied.

"I disagree," his son retorted. "And, what is more, I wish to have no part in it."

Sir Edward brought his fist down violently on the table and in that moment he became galvanised into a dynamic force.

"What do you mean, you'll have no part in it? You'll do as I say. Am I the head of this firm or am I not? Am I thinking of our best interests and also your future, or am I going to mess up what is one of the biggest things that have ever come our way in the whole life-time of trading?"

Ian Blakewell shrugged his shoulders and turning from the desk walked almost petulantly towards the window.

'What a disagreeable young man he is,' Varia thought to herself.

She felt almost sympathetic to Sir Edward because it was obvious that he was sincerely convinced that what he wanted to do was the right thing, while the younger man

17

merely seemed obstructive.

"I must apologise, Miss Milfield," Sir Edward said with a sudden, old-world courtesy. "My son and I are having a little argument and we have been rude enough to ignore that you have joined us. Won't you come and sit down?"

A little embarrassed, Varia seated herself on the chair he indicated on the other side of the desk. Sir Edward looked at her and she looked at Sir Edward and she found, to her surprise, that they were both smiling.

"You are very like your mother, my dear," Sir Edward said quietly.

"My mother!" Varia ejaculated.

She had expected, when she came to the office, to hear something unusual, but certainly not this.

"Yes, very like her," Sir Edward said. "In fact, looking at you I might be stepping back twenty-five years into the past."

"You knew my mother then?" Varia asked.

"Yes, indeed," Sir Edward said. "I remember her very well indeed and I think perhaps she will remember me."

"I must ask her," Varia said. "She didn't say when I told her where I was working, that she had ever met you."

"As it happens, she would not know me

by the name of Blakewell," Sir Edward said. "My uncle on my mother's side left me a considerable sum of money about five years after I knew your mother, on condition that I change my name to his."

"Oh, I see," Varia said.

There was a sudden silence while Sir Edward stared at her, and yet she had a feeling that he was not seeing her but her mother.

'What did all this mean?' she wondered, and almost ventured a question of her own when Ian Blakewell turned from the window.

"Really, Father! I think we should discuss this again without Miss Milfield being present."

"What I have to say concerns Miss Milfield and therefore I wish her to be here," Sir Edward replied.

Varia looked from one to the other, perplexed. Ian Blakewell was scowling and as his eyes met hers the frown between them grew even deeper.

'I believe he dislikes me,' Varia thought. 'Why? Why?'

"Miss Milfield, I will come to the point," Sir Edward said, "and that is that I have asked you here to know if you will do the firm a great service."

"But, of course!" Varia replied. "If it is something I can do."

"You can help us in an unusual and certainly, I think, unique way," Sir Edward said.

"Father, I beg you . . ." Ian Blakewell interjected.

"Will you be quiet!" Sir Edward said sharply. "Let me handle this in my own manner."

He turned again to Varia.

"I am going to explain to you very briefly," he said, "the situation in which we find ourselves. You know, having worked here for some months, that we are the oldest and the largest importers of silk in this country."

Varia nodded and he went on:

"We do not manufacture but we have, in the last few years, set up a laboratory to make certain experiments in the treatment of silk and the preservation of it. It was a side line in which I became interested, perhaps ten years ago, and was always considered a sheer waste of money by the rest of the directors and, in particular, by my son."

He shot a glance at Ian who had seated himself now at the other desk and was obviously engaged in doodling on the blotting paper with a pencil.

He did not look up, but Varia realised that he was listening tensely and she was convinced, hating every word of what he heard.

"My investigations were, however, not as fruitless as might have been anticipated," Sir Edward went on. "In fact, the scientists I engaged have discovered a new process which will, when put into use, completely revolutionise the silk trade.

"To put it briefly so that you can understand it, my dear, we have invented something which will not only preserve silk and prevent it from deteriorating or becoming discoloured, but will also prevent it from creasing however badly or roughly it is handled."

"How wonderful!" Varia exclaimed.

"Yes, indeed, it is wonderful," Sir Edward agreed. "And that is what all those who are anxious to buy our process apparently think."

He shot another glance at his son and then went on:

"You will understand, Miss Milfield, that there is going to be very hot competition for this particular invention, but we are, in fact, morally bound to offer it first to the silk merchants from whom the great majority of our importations come — Duflot in Lyons."

"Oh, yes! I've heard their name," Varia said.

"If you worked here even for a day you would have heard it," Sir Edward told her, "because our businesses are as closely linked as two businesses possibly could be. Monsieur François Duflot has been a faithful and loyal associate of ours and I have the greatest respect for his business ability."

"Yes, of course," Varia said, feeling that something was expected of her, but wondering where his story was leading.

"And now I come to the point," Sir Edward said. "Monsieur Duflot has agreed to take over this process from us, to use it in his Company's factories and to let us have the exclusive right to import every piece of silk that they treat in this manner. Now you understand what that means?"

"Yes, I think so," Varia said a little doubtfully.

"It means," Sir Edward said impressively, "that as we shall be the sole importers everyone in the British Isles will have to come to us if they wish to buy this particular sort of silk that has been treated by the Blakewell method."

"But how wonderful for you!" Varia smiled.

"Wonderful, indeed," Sir Edward agreed. "But there is a snag."

"Father! I beg you . . ." Ian interrupted.

Sir Edward ignored him.

"The snag is that to be quite certain there is no question of us letting anyone but the Duflot Company have this clever invention, Monsieur Duflot has suggested an even closer alliance between our two families. He wishes, in fact, for my son to marry his daughter."

"Oh!"

The ejaculation came spontaneously from Varia's lips. She began to understand now what all the argument was about.

"You see, my dear," Sir Edward went on. "On the Continent they do arrange these things. I know the French very well and although they have become slightly more emancipated in the past few years, in all the solid business families, as well as in many aristocratic circles, *mariages de convenance* are still arranged as a matter of course."

He paused, then continued.

"It means that each family gains something by the marriage, and it completely eliminates any of these *mésalliances* which happen so often amongst our friends and even in our own families."

"But, if . . . people don't love each other . . ." Varia faltered.

"Love! That is the English point of view," Sir Edward answered. "Love comes very often when two people are ably suited and when they have the same interests. And if it doesn't — well, the French expect both husband and wife to amuse themselves so long as there is no scandal."

"It doesn't sound . . . to me a very . . . happy idea," Varia faltered.

"Perhaps you are right," Sir Edward replied. "Anyway, such arrangements are obviously repugnant to English people. But, here is the difficulty. I cannot offend my old friend, François Duflot, by telling him that my son will not under any circumstances contemplate marrying his daughter."

"Would he be very offended?" Varia asked.

"He would not only be offended," Sir Edward replied. "He would not understand."

"Then you should make him," Ian Blakewell interposed.

"My dear Ian, one cannot change a man. François has great points. Where business is concerned there is no-one shrewder, more intelligent or more progressive. But as a middle-class Frenchman, that is a very dif-

24

ferent thing. He does not understand our customs."

Sir Edward sighed before he continued:

"I could not make him see that you do not wish to marry as a matter of principle. He would take it as a personal insult — so personal, indeed, that our business arrangement together would be affected."

"It's fantastic! Impossible!" Ian Blakewell exclaimed angrily.

"When you have seen François Duflot in his own home, then you will understand," Sir Edward said coldly. "And now, Miss Milfield — or may I perhaps call you Varia because I knew your mother many years ago? — I will get down to business."

"To business!" Varia echoed in a bewildered tone.

"Yes! This is where I want you to help us," Sir Edward said. "My son has to go to France to arrange the contracts between Blakewell and Duflot. I want you to go with him."

"But am I experienced enough?" Varia asked. "I'm not very good at shorthand."

"I'm not asking you to go as a secretary," Sir Edward replied. "I'm asking you to go as my son's future wife!"

Varia opened her mouth to speak but no sound came. For a moment she just stared at Sir Edward, thinking he had taken leave of his senses. And then, as he saw her face, he exclaimed quickly:

"Unofficially, of course, and as far as we are concerned, this will be entirely a business arrangement. I have thought it all out. I will write saying that my son is bringing with him his future wife although the engagement is not yet announced publicly. You will spend a week there and then return to this country."

His voice changed as he went on: "Later — perhaps one month — perhaps two months later, I shall write to François Duflot and tell him that the engagement is unfortunately terminated as it is felt you are not temperamentally suited. What do you think of my idea?"

"But . . . I don't know what to say," Varia answered a little helplessly, looking from Sir Edward to the scowling young man across the other side of the room.

"As far as I'm concerned you can tell my father it is quite ridiculous," Ian Blakewell said in a hostile tone. "It is an insult to you and — to me. If François is so old-fashioned and out of date that he doesn't understand that a man wants to choose his own wife, then it's about time he learned that other people in other countries have a

26

more sensible outlook."

"Ian! Ian! We have been over this before," Sir Edward snapped. "You know what it means to us to have the biggest and most influential firm in France take up our invention. We cannot throw this away for the sake of some silly prejudice on your part."

Ian Blakewell did not answer and Sir Edward turned to Varia.

"Will you do this for the firm?" he said. "Will you do it for me? And, most of all, will you do it for your mother?"

"For my mother?" Varia questioned.

Sir Edward looked down at his desk. For a moment she fancied he was embarrassed.

"I have taken the trouble to find out your position," he said. "I have learned of your father's death and of your mother's illness. I have found out, too, that she is not having all the comforts she needs."

Varia flushed crimson.

"We cannot . . . afford them," she stammered.

"I know that," Sir Edward answered. "That is why I was going to suggest that if you will do this for me, I will pay you for your services one thousand pounds!"

"As . . . much as that!" Varia exclaimed.

"It is not very much for what we shall gain in return," Sir Edward replied. "But I think you would be able to help your mother, perhaps, to better health."

"She could go to Switzerland," Varia said almost beneath her breath. "The Doctor spoke of it. We all knew it was . . . impossible."

"Yes, she could go to Switzerland," Sir Edward agreed.

Varia drew a deep breath and then said suddenly:

"But I don't think she would agree. I don't think she would allow me to do this even if I were willing."

"Must you tell her?" Sir Edward enquired.

Varia felt her heart leap at the idea Sir Edward presented to her. Her mother could go to Switzerland. A month out there might make all the difference; the Doctor had said so.

Perhaps her mother need never know how she got there. Perhaps she could concoct some wonderful fund that had come forward to assist her. Her mother was so ill that she wouldn't ask many questions.

A thousand pounds! It was a fortune!

"Perhaps you've guessed," Sir Edward said quietly, "that once I loved your mother. She refused to marry me because she was already in love with your father and because, too, I was not worthy of her. But I have never forgotten her — never!"

He spoke in a low voice almost as if he wished his son not to hear.

Ian Blakewell was still drawing on the blotting paper. Quite suddenly he threw the pencil down with an irritated, angry gesture. Then he looked up and Varia met his eyes.

She felt something disturbing and antagonistic pass between them. There was a hostility which was almost alive it was so violent.

He was challenging her, she thought, and knew in that moment that she had made up her mind.

She turned defiantly towards Sir Edward.

"Thank you," she said quietly. "I will accept your proposition and I will go to France with your son."

Varia looked round the little mews flat which had been her home for nearly six years and thought how empty it seemed.

Her mother had left by air that morning for Switzerland and Varia had watched the aeroplane out of sight with tears in her eyes. They had been tears of joy, the joy of knowing that she had been able to provide what the Doctor had called "a quite reasonable chance of recovery" for her mother.

It was the Doctor who decided that everything should be done quickly. He had telephoned the sanatorium in Lausanne, arranged for Mrs. Milfield's passport and ticket and ordered an ambulance to take her to the aerodrome.

Never had Varia been so glad of anything as to have enough money to ensure that the journey itself was comfortable and that everything possible was provided.

Only when she came back alone to the mews flat did she begin once again to think of herself, to remember that this had all got to be paid for by her Journey to France with Ian Blakewell.

She felt a sudden little sinking of the heart as she looked round the familiar flat and remembered that she had made an engagement to meet Sir Edward Blakewell at three o'clock.

She had another job to perform this afternoon and that was to take Fluff to stay with Ted Huggins until her mother returned.

She knew how excited the frail little boy would be, but it would be a perfect solution to the problem of what to do with Fluff while she was in France.

"Come on, Fluff," she said as he sat watching her, his funny little white head cocked to one side.

It was only as they crossed Kensington High Street that Varia found herself thinking of the Frenchman to whom Fluff had introduced her at the beginning of the week.

'Was it only four days ago?' she wondered. It seemed impossible. So much had happened since then and she felt as if an aeon of time had passed since she last came this way into the Park.

"Go home. Make arrangements to get your mother to Switzerland, and then come back and see me on Thursday afternoon," Sir Edward had commanded.

"Shall I . . . say anything in the . . . office?" Varia had stammered, thinking of Miss Crankshaft's disapproving face and of the girls' curiosity.

"No, nothing," Sir Edward said. "We don't want a lot of gossip."

Varia was so deep in her thoughts now that it was only Fluff's yelping and pulling at the lead which reminded her that she had reached the part of the Park where he was allowed to go free. She bent down to undo the lead when a voice beside her said:

"At last I've found you again."

She looked up and saw, with a surprising lack of astonishment, that the Frenchman stood there — Pierre de Chalayat.

31

"Hello!" she said, and knew, as she said it, that some sixth sense within her had known that he would be there.

"Where have you been?" he demanded. "I have been here every morning; I have come here every afternoon. I began to think that I had just imagined you, that you never existed."

"I have been busy," Varia answered, but her eyes fell before his and she felt the colour rise just a little within her cheeks.

"But, how could you be so cruel?" he asked. "Did you not know that I should want to see you again?"

"How could I know it?" she replied. "After all, we were just strangers who met by chance."

"Do you really believe it was chance?" he asked. "Do you not think that it was planned since the very beginning of time that you and I should meet on just that spot?"

Varia found herself being hypnotised by the almost irresistible attraction of his voice. With an effort she forced herself to answer lightly:

"I think you are talking nonsense," she said. "And really we ought not to be talking at all. You know quite well that all nice girls have been warned about picking up strange men in the Park."

"I know! I know!" he said. "But I am not a strange man any more. I am Pierre! Do you remember? Pierre, who has been thinking about you, looking for you and longing for you for four days. Come and sit down for a moment," he begged.

Varia glanced at her wrist-watch. It was not quite twenty-to-three.

"Only for a few minutes," she said. "I have an appointment at three o'clock."

"Where?" he asked.

"At the office where I work," she answered. "It's just off Park Lane. It won't take me long to get there."

"And when you have been to the office, what then?" Pierre enquired. "Where can I meet you? Will you dine with me tonight?"

"Oh, I don't think I can do that," Varia answered.

"Why not?" he asked. "Am I repulsive to you?"

"No, no," Varia replied, a little embarrassed by such a direct question. "Perhaps I am being stupid. It is just that I have never met anyone like you before — in fact, as it happens, I have never dined out alone with anyone."

"*C'est impossible!*" Pierre seemed really astonished. "But, why? Do you live in a convent or something? Or have the men of England got no eyes?"

"Well, as it happens," Varia answered, "I haven't been grown up a very long time. My mother has been ill for some time and we don't know many people in London, and so I have always dined at home."

"Where is your home?"

Even as he asked the question Varia decided not to tell him. There was some cautious streak within her which held her back from being swept along on the tide of the Frenchman's enthusiasm and charm.

"Not very far from here," she answered. "And, now, I really must go."

"I will walk with you," he said.

"Only as far as Stanhope Gate," she parried.

She had a feeling that it would be very unwise to let Sir Edward, or Ian Blakewell for that matter, see her arrive at the door of the office with an attractive young man.

"All right, as far as Stanhope Gate," Pierre answered. "So long as you promise that you will dine with me tonight."

"Very well, it is a bargain. I will dine with you," Varia said.

"May I fetch you?" he asked.

She shook her head.

"No! I think I would rather meet you at

the restaurant. Where are you thinking of taking me?"

"I think somewhere small and intimate where we can talk," Pierre said. "There is a lot I want to tell you. There is a lot I want you to tell me."

He hesitated for a moment and then said:

"I know. *Le Chat Gris* is a rather amusing French restaurant that has just opened in Jermyn Street. Will you meet me there at eight o'clock?"

"Very well," Varia answered, feeling in some extraordinary way that she was committing herself to something, wanting to go and yet at the same time half afraid to do so.

"You promise you'll come?" Pierre was saying. "Promise me that you will not disappear again."

"I promise," Varia answered.

"If you only knew what I have been through these last days. One day perhaps I will make you understand."

"I cannot think why you should be so interested."

She was not being coquettish, she was just being friendly, and in answer he stopped suddenly still and took both her hands in his.

"Listen, Varia," he said. "I am a great be-
liever in Fate. All my life things have happened to me and I have known that there
was some plan behind them. When I looked
up into your face from where I had fallen to
the ground, I was aware that something mo-
mentous had happened, something I should
never forget. Have you any idea how adorable you are?"

Varia blushed and tried to take her hands
away from his, but he held on to them.

"No, listen to me for a moment. I had no
idea that anyone could have eyes that were
really the colour of the spring violets, eyes
which hold a special magic for me and yet,
at the same time, seem as shy as the little
flowers that peep beneath their leaves at the
first awakening of the spring."

If an Englishman had said such things
Varia would have thought him ridiculous.
But when they were said with Pierre's fasci-
nating French accent, spoken in his crisp,
compelling voice, she found herself caught
up into a kind of magic spell from which she
could not break away.

"So young, so unawakened, so utterly enchanting!" he added softly.

His eyes were on her lips for a moment
and she felt almost as if his mouth touched
hers.

Then, dragging herself free of him, she was hurrying away with Fluff on his lead, her cheeks burning, refusing to look back even as she heard him call after her.

"Eight o'clock, *Le Chat Gris*! Don't forget, Varia. Please don't forget."

'I am crazy,' she thought. 'Crazy to listen to him; still more crazy to go. Oh, dear! Why is everything happening to me all at once? It is all so exciting, and yet rather frightening at the same time.'

The policeman held up the traffic and she hurried across Park Lane. It was not yet three o'clock. She was punctual and she also had time to take Fluff down to Ted. She hurried down to the basement.

The little boy, who was making a slow recovery after suffering a spinal injury, was overjoyed to be in charge of Fluff. Varia left them together and went upstairs to Sir Edward's office.

She knocked on the door. For a moment there wasn't an answer and then a voice said abruptly:

"Come in!"

As she entered the room, she saw that the big desk facing the door was empty. Sir Edward was not there, but Ian Blakewell was seated at the other desk with his back to the window.

He rose slowly to his feet.

"Good afternoon!" he said uncompromisingly.

"Good afternoon!" Varia answered. "You . . . you were expecting me?"

"Yes, of course," Ian Blakewell said. "Won't you sit down? I am afraid my father will be unable to come here this afternoon. He sent his instructions through me."

Varia sat still and waited. As if he, too, felt ill at ease, Ian Blakewell sat down rather awkwardly in his chair and picking up an ivory paper-knife, turned it over and over in his fingers.

"There are quite a lot of things to be done," he said. "And unfortunately there is only a very short time to do them because my father wishes us to leave for France tomorrow. Our seats are booked on the afternoon plane."

There was a pause while Varia waited, expecting him to say something more. After a moment he said with an effort:

"I . . . I'll pick you up about quarter-past-one, if that will be convenient."

"Oh, perfectly convenient," Varia said.

Again there was a pause while Ian Blakewell went on turning over the paper-knife. Varia somehow felt it was up to her to make a move.

"Well, if that's everything, Mr. Blakewell . . ." she began.

"Wait a minute!" he interrupted. "My father asked me to discuss something with you. You see, he thought that you might not have exactly the right type of clothes which would be necessary for a journey such as this and he has therefore made arrangements for you."

"What sort of arrangements?"

"For you to have a kind of trousseau of the sort of things that would be expected of you as my future wife," Ian Blakewell said bluntly.

"Oh, but I don't think . . ." Varia began, only to stop and look at him. "I don't think . . ." she began again, and then finished, "that I ought to take clothes. I mean, I can buy them myself out of the thousand pounds that your father has already paid me."

"He doesn't wish you to do that," Ian Blakewell said. "In fact, he has made an appointment for you to go to a shop where you will be completely fitted out with the right things."

Varia sat very still. This was something she had not anticipated. In fact, in the flurry and excitement of getting her mother off to Switzerland, she had really forgotten about her clothes.

Now, thinking of her worn coat and skirt, of the plain, cheap afternoon dress that she wore on Sundays and on better occasions, of her absolute lack of evening frocks, she realised how dense she had been.

Of course she couldn't go to France like that. Why, they would think it extraordinary — if they didn't suspect immediately — that young Blakewell with all his money was making a very bad *mésalliance* in marrying such a poverty-stricken girl.

"I think that your father is quite right," she said a little hastily. "I had really forgotten how inadequate my wardrobe would be. But I think I ought to use some of the money he has already given me."

"That is quite unnecessary," Ian Blakewell said. "My father is prepared to write the clothes off as part of your expenses. It would be no more sensible for you to pay for those than to pay for your ticket on the aeroplane."

He spoke almost harshly and Varia thought once again there was an expression of dislike and disdain on his face as if he despised her from the very bottom of his heart. She felt her irritation at him rise.

There was no need for him to be so aggressive. He might guess that this was embarrassing for her.

"Very well then," she said abruptly. "I shall be pleased to accept whatever arrangements your father has made. Please thank him for me."

"I'll do that," Ian Blakewell said. "And now I will take you along to the shop. Its owner happens to be a friend of my father."

He rose to his feet and Varia remained seated.

"Listen, Mr. Blakewell," she said. "If you hate the idea of this so much, would you rather refuse to do it? I see no point in going to France if we are going to make a failure of it."

"Do you think we shall?" Ian Blakewell asked.

"Well, they are certainly going to think it strange that we are supposed to be engaged when you glare at me as you are doing now," Varia retorted.

Even as she spoke the words she felt her heart beat with astonishment at her own courage. She would not have dreamed a week ago of speaking to anyone — let alone Ian Blakewell — in such a manner. But somehow he stung her into doing it.

"I am sorry," Ian Blakewell said quickly. "I suppose I am behaving boorishly. But quite frankly, as you know, I hate the whole idea."

41

"All the same, I can understand your father's point of view," Varia told him. "If you don't want to marry Mademoiselle Duflot or to have the discomfort of having to say so, it does seem to be the most tactful way of getting out of what might be a very uncomfortable situation."

"Then I suppose I must be wrong," he said. "To me . . . Oh, what's the use of talking. I've gone over this with my father innumerable times. Very well, we must make the best of it."

She followed him as he walked across the room to open the door and they went out together to where his Bentley was waiting.

"We haven't got much time," he said. "There's a great deal to be done before two-thirty tomorrow."

They drove in silence through the crowded streets and then he drew up outside a big house with a red awning on which there was displayed a name that made Varia open her eyes in surprise.

"Is this where we are going?" she asked.

"Yes, do you know it?" Ian Blakewell asked.

"I've heard of it, of course," Varia answered. "Who hasn't heard of Martin Myles? But does your father really mean me to have clothes from here?"

"That is what he has arranged," Ian Blakewell said.

They got out of the car and walked under the awning and in through the big, open front door.

There were stairs covered in pale dove-grey carpet leading to the first floor; there were pillars of iridescent-looking glass; there were glittering crystal chandeliers.

Varia was too awed to speak; and then, as they entered an enormous, brightly lit Salon, a woman dressed in pale mauve, with her hair apparently dyed to match, came hurrying forward.

"Good afternoon, Mr. Blakewell," she said. "We are expecting you. Mr. Myles said will you come into his private office?"

The most important designer of women's clothes in Great Britain rose from a desk covered with designs and held out his hand.

He was quite a young man, thin and pale, with untidy fair hair, horn-rimmed spectacles and a rather harassed expression.

"Ian, my dear fellow," he exclaimed. "I'm delighted to see you. But your father has been bullying me all day on the telephone, until I feel quite distraught as to what is expected of me."

"How are you, Martin?" Ian said, and added abruptly: "This is Miss Milfield."

Varia realised that Mr. Myles' eyes belied his appearance. They were practical in their way. They swept over her. She felt every part of her was revealed mercilessly and uncompromisingly to his inspection.

He said nothing and she felt she was waiting for the verdict from some supreme judge. Then, unexpectedly, he smiled.

"All that your father expects is quite possible," he said to Ian. Then turning to her, he asked: "But where, Miss Milfield, did you buy that appalling coat and skirt?"

His question was so unexpected that Varia found herself blushing and stammering.

"I . . . I've had it a . . . long time."

"I don't doubt it," Mr. Myles replied. "It is not only out of fashion, it has never been in it. Throw it away; throw it away at once!"

Varia stood helplessly wondering what to do, and the woman in mauve, who had brought them to the room, came to her rescue.

"You are being naughty, Mr. Myles," she said. "You are making poor Miss Milfield quite embarrassed. Let me get her a chair and we can show her the things which we have planned for her to have out of our collection."

She brought forward a chair and Varia sank thankfully into it.

"Now, Madame René," Mr. Myles said, "we must decide which are the most suitable of these two."

He pushed forward two designs — one of a pale rose-coloured dress of tulle ornamented with roses; the other of tulle in the palest shade of turquoise with exquisite embroidery on the bodice and on the scarf which encircled the shoulders.

Finally, after a great deal of argument in which neither she nor Ian Blakewell took part, Varia was ushered into a fitting-room where dress after dress was brought and tried on her.

To her delight and secret satisfaction she was model size — her waist was perfect and so was her bust; only in some cases was a dress a little too long.

"I can't be having all these, surely," she said at length in an awed voice, as about the twentieth dress was put over her head and she was zipped into it.

Madame René consulted the list.

"No, there are three afternoon dresses," she said. "But Mr. Myles wants to be quite certain that you do him credit."

She opened the door as she spoke and Mr. Myles, who went tactfully from the fitting-room between every change of costume, entered.

"Charming!" he said. "That colour suits her. It is a pity that she cannot have the organza as well, but I think this will be more suitable."

After a time she began to grow tired. It was wonderful to see herself looking so different, but the room was hot and peculiarly airless.

She glanced at her watch and saw that already it was half-past-six. An hour-and-a-half before she had to be at *Le Chat Gris*. She felt herself looking forward to dining out with an intensity that was almost frightening. She mustn't be so eager and so pleased. After all, she had only just met the man and after tonight she might never see him again.

"Well, that is the lot," she suddenly heard Mr. Myles say. "Have the alterations made and get them all pressed and round to Miss Milfield's house by eleven o'clock tomorrow. That will give you time to pack them, won't it?" he asked.

"But I haven't got anything to pack them in," Varia said.

Madame René rose to the occasion.

"Do not worry," she said. "We will lend you some suitcases. You certainly won't have time to go and buy any."

"No, I am afraid the shops will be closed

now, at any rate," Varia replied.

"Not the shops I am taking you to. They are being kept specially open," Madame René smiled.

"But what else could I want?" Varia enquired.

"Hats, for one thing; underclothes for another. And then, of course, there is your hair."

Varia looked in the glass.

"I thought my hair was all right," she said. "I washed it two days ago."

Madame René gave her a glance out of her over-mascara'd eyes and Varia felt herself blush. Of course, they didn't think her hair style was good enough.

Then she remembered the time.

"But . . . but I had no idea this was to happen. I have got to meet . . . someone at eight o'clock."

"Then you had better telephone and put them off," Ian Blakewell said.

"I . . . I don't think I can . . ." Varia began, and then saw that he was smiling at her in what she thought was a hateful triumphant way.

"It's not so easy to make the best of it, is it, when it cuts across one's own inclinations?" he asked.

Her eyes met his and she had the insane

desire to shout at him:

"You hate me and I hate you."

She wanted to say: "Very well, if you want to do this fighting, I'll fight you!"

But she said nothing. Instead she turned on her heel and walked from the room, hating him with an intensity that was almost unbearable because she had never hated anyone before.

Chapter Two

Afterwards Varia could never quite remember what had happened in the next three hours.

She was taken from Martin Myles' shop to a milliner's where she met Erik, a tall blond Scandinavian who she learned, to her surprise, was the designer of the delectable creations which were arranged on green wooden perches as if they were exotic birds.

Erik's lovely, unusual, exciting hats, were put on her head and taken off again.

She stood, and sat, she turned round obediently at every request, becoming more and more like an automaton until finally it was with a sense of utter relief that she realised that they were once more driving in Ian Blakewell's car to another destination.

They drew up outside a hairdresser's. The shops on either side were closed, but Varia could read the word *Vincent* in gold letters on a green awning. She could also see bright lights shining through the open door and uncurtained window.

"I will come back for you in an hour-and-a-half," Ian Blakewell said to Madame René. "And then I had better take you both to have something to eat."

Varia was whisked into a cubicle; she slipped her arms into a wrapper of pale blue nylon; and then Mr. Vincent was behind her, snipping away at her hair, altering the shape until, as she watched him in the glass, she began to wonder if she would be able to recognise herself again.

Even before Vincent had finished, she could see the improvement. Her hair — spun gold though it was in colour — had looked heavy and often untidy.

Now it was light and neat, and at the same time the line from the top of her head to her white rounded neck was exquisite.

"C'est ravissant, Vincent!" she heard Madame René say.

Then her hair was being washed and she was taken from the basin to sit in front of a huge mirror lit by the Venetian glass wall brackets, while Mr. Vincent set her hair into innumerable small silver clips.

It was at this moment that she realised that it was already twenty-past-eight. She stared at her watch, feeling a sudden stab of pain and with it a sense of loss and desolation.

There was nothing she could do, nothing, except to telephone and tell him that she could not come.

Suddenly shy and tongue-tied, it took all her courage to say aloud:

"Could I . . . telephone?"

"But certainly," Mr. Vincent smiled.

Going to a desk nearby, he brought back a telephone on a long flex and set it down beside her.

"I shall want the . . . the . . . telephone book, I'm afraid," she faltered.

Mr. Vincent fetched it for her.

"Shall I look it up for you?" Madame René asked.

"No, it's all . . . right, thank you," Varia answered, turning over the pages until she found *Le Chat Gris*.

She dialled the number and waited, and then as she listened for a voice to answer, she was suddenly conscious of the two people beside her.

She had never met them before today and she felt shy and embarrassed that they should overhear her conversation with Pierre.

" 'Ello! 'Ello!"

There was a foreigner at the other end of the telephone.

51

"Is that . . . *Le Chat Gris?*" Varia enquired. "Could I . . . ? No, could you . . . give a message to . . . Monsieur Pierre de Chalayat?"

"Comte Pierre is here, Madame," the voice replied. "Would you like to speak to him?"

"No, no," Varia answered quickly.

Somehow she could not face it, could not speak to him when Madame René and Mr. Vincent were listening.

"Will you tell him, please, that . . . Miss Milfield is very sorry but . . . she cannot come . . . this evening. Tell him also that she is . . . leaving for France . . . tomorrow."

"Miss Milfield cannot come this evening and is leaving for France tomorrow. Is that right, Madame?"

"Yes, that's . . . right," Varia replied in a flat voice. She did not know why, but she felt as if she had thrown away something infinitely precious. It was gone! There was nothing she could do about it.

"Thank . . . you," she said. "Thank you very much."

She put the receiver down.

Had she been stupid not to speak to Pierre? she wondered. It would have been some consolation at least to have heard him express his disappointment.

No, no, it was all too complicated. Besides, in her heart of hearts she was a little afraid of his openly expressed admiration. It was no use thinking of Pierre, or any man like him, at this moment when she had her job to do, and she had got to do it well.

It was bad enough to accept a thousand pounds, but still worse even to guess what her clothes must have cost! There were also her hats and all the other things which Madame René had told her would be at her flat tomorrow morning.

While she was still with Martin Myles her feet had been measured for shoes, and Madame René had also told her that an order had been given for underclothes, nightgowns, bags and gloves, all of which were being sent to the flat.

Her thoughts were still in a whirl when Mr. Vincent at last turned off the dryer. He then began to brush her hair.

Varia had thought she looked different after he had finished cutting her hair, but now she was amazed at her appearance.

Her hair was shining like living gold, but what was much more surprising was the difference its new shape made to her appearance. She looked younger in a way and yet there was an air of sophistication about her that had not been there before.

"Thank you so very much," she said in her soft voice, holding out her hand.

"I hope you have a lovely time in France," Mr. Vincent smiled. "At least there will be no-one on either side of the Channel to equal your looks."

Varia smiled a little shyly at the compliment and then followed Madame René to the door. The big grey Bentley was standing outside. Ian Blakewell was seated at the wheel looking bored.

"I'm afraid we've kept you waiting," Madame René said.

"Don't bother to apologise," he answered. "I'm used to it. I telephoned my father and told him everything had been done as he ordered, and he now insists that we have dinner at the Berkeley Grill."

"Oh, but I'm sure . . ." Varia began, only to stop as they both looked at her.

"I'm sorry," she added in confusion, "but I . . . I thought we ought to go . . . somewhere quiet. You see, I'm not dressed . . ."

"It doesn't matter what you look like," Ian Blakewell said quickly before Madame René could speak. "What we all want is something to eat."

He drove off quickly and Varia sat in the corner of the car feeling snubbed. She had not expected anything but dislike from him.

At the same time, it was depressing to think that, however she looked, however different she appeared, he would always address her with that coldness in his voice, the dislike in his eyes.

Pierre was so different. If only Pierre could have seen her with her hair like this, she thought. If only Pierre could see her in her new clothes.

She thought of the look which would come into his eyes. Those bold eyes which made her think of buccaneers who captured by force what they desired.

"I thought I had lost you!" She could hear his voice, deep, low and strangely compelling . . .

"Here we are!" Madame René exclaimed.

Varia gave a start. She had been far away from reality and had actually forgotten where she was.

Ian parked the Bentley and they walked in through the revolving doors. It was late, but even so there were quite a number of people still sitting at the tables in the cool, green-walled Grill.

"I'm Mr. Blakewell," Ian said to the head-waiter.

"Your table is reserved, Sir. Will you come this way?"

He led them to a table which had a comfortable sofa instead of chairs, and brought them each a large menu which to Varia seemed utterly incomprehensible.

"I think we'll have a little champagne," Ian said. "I'm sure my father would consider that this calls for a celebration."

There was a tinge of bitterness in his voice, but Madame René seemed not to notice it.

"I heard Mr. Myles say that you are both going to Lyons tomorrow," she said. "How I envy you! My home is in that part of France — not in Lyons, but in Montelimar. I live in England because I am married to an Englishman, but I go back every summer to see my parents."

"I don't know Lyons, as a matter of fact," Ian Blakewell said. "I have motored through it on the way to Monte Carlo but I remember Montelimar. I remember being taken to buy the nougat there when I was a little boy."

"Ah! It is delicious, *n'est-ce pas?*" Madame René cried.

They talked on, seeming, Varia thought, to ignore her until finally dinner was finished and Ian called for the bill.

As he did so, the door leading from the hotel opened and a woman came into the restaurant. She was wearing a draped gown of dead white crêpe.

There was a stole of white mink round her shoulders and her red hair was swept forward in elaborate carelessness over her square forehead.

She walked in in a dramatically graceful manner which showed that she had been taught to move with a studied elegance.

When she reached the centre of the room she turned, looked around her, and saw Ian. She came across to the table and Varia thought she was the most striking person she had ever seen in her life.

She was lovely, but her beauty was sensational, like a modernistic painting.

Her white skin, green eyes beneath heavily shaded lids and a very full, painted mouth, gave her the look almost of a sorceress or perhaps of a witch as mankind has always dreamed one might be.

"Ian! So this is where you are hiding!" she said accusingly as she reached the table.

He rose hastily to his feet.

"I'm sorry, Lareen, that I couldn't come tonight. I did my best, but it was impossible."

The redhead's green eyes turned towards Madame René.

"Hello!" she said a little uncompromisingly, and then looked at Varia. "Is this what stopped you?"

"I don't think you've met Miss Milfield," Ian said hastily. "Miss Milfield — Miss Lareen Gilmay!"

As soon as she heard the name of the girl facing her. Varia knew who she was. It was impossible to pick up any newspaper without seeing her face in the advertisements.

The famous model of expensive productions; a girl who reputedly had risen in a few months to own the most photographed face in the whole of Great Britain.

"How do you do!"

Lareen's green eyes were hostile and her nod to Varia was barely civil. Turning to Ian, she said in a low voice:

"How could you? You promised to come and I didn't expect you to fail me."

"I couldn't help it," he said. "I had something to do for my father."

"Sir Edward again!" Lareen made a little grimace which was, Varia thought, irresistibly attractive. "Must your father always be the excuse?"

"It appears so," Ian replied.

"Well, I may forgive you if you will take me racing tomorrow. I want to go to Sandown. Jimmy has a horse running."

"I'm afraid that's impossible," Ian answered. "I'm off to France tomorrow."

"To France!" Lareen made the words a cry of protest. "You can't be! You know we've made plans to go to Marjorie for the week-end."

"I'm sorry. I tried to reach you on the telephone yesterday to explain that I could not get out of my father's arrangements. I tried. I spoke to him again last night; but he wouldn't budge."

"Are you a man or a mouse?" Lareen asked with a curl of her lip. "Ah, well! There are other people. David has been dying to take me, as it happened, but I told him I had promised to go with you. *Au revoir,* Ian! Let me know when you come back from your trip. I feel sure you'll enjoy it."

There was a sting in her voice that was unmistakable as she turned on her heel and, leaving behind a whiff of expensive perfume, moved back towards the door through which she had come.

"Lareen! Wait!" Ian called, and hurried after her.

Varia saw him take her arm and they went out through the door together, he speaking animatedly and Lareen shrugging her shoulders with an asperity which was quite obvious to anyone watching them.

"She is very beautiful," Varia said in an awed voice.

"She's a nasty little vixen," Madame René retorted.

Varia looked at her in surprise.

"Yes, I mean what I say," Madame René said. "I know Lareen well. It was Mr. Myles who made her, for that matter. He saw her in some obscure beauty competition in Birmingham or Manchester, I cannot remember which. He brought her to London, had her taught how to walk, how to speak and how to wear clothes."

Madame René gave a little snort.

"She learnt quickly enough! She was a success and it went to her head. If ever there was a young woman who has been spoilt by applause it's Lareen Gilmay."

"She's so beautiful!" Varia repeated, feeling that someone as lovely could not be wholly bad.

Madame René sighed.

"I see a lot of beautiful women one way and another," she said. "But one can get very tired of beauty when it is nothing but a pretty face. In my country they say — *'le coeur, c'est tout'* — the heart is all. That is what so many people forget. If your heart is lovely, you cannot really be ugly whatever your face may be like. If you have no heart, then the prettiest face isn't worth looking at."

"I know what you mean," Varia said. "Mummy always warns me not to be carried away by appearances, but I find it very difficult not to be."

"You will learn as you grow older," Madame René told her. "And so, I expect, will Mr. Blakewell."

"Do you think he is really in love with her?" Varia asked.

"No! People aren't really in love with Lareen," Madame René answered. "She hypnotises them for a little while with that theatrical appearance which they think is glamorous but underneath she's got a nasty, common little back-street mind which would nauseate anyone if they got a really good look at it."

Madame René's lips tightened.

"I have seen the dirty tricks she can play on the other girls who are earning their living," she said. "I have seen her cheat to get her own way and to do down some other poor wretch just for the sheer love of showing off her power. Lareen is a bad girl and bad girls usually get found out sooner or later."

Varia listened, fascinated. She felt that Madame René was opening windows on to a world that she never knew existed, and yet she could not help thinking how beautiful and unusual Lareen was.

She could understand Ian Blakewell being in love with her — for whatever Madame René might say to the contrary, that, she was sure, was the truth.

'And why shouldn't he be?' Varia asked herself.

Now she began to understand why he was so angry with his father, why he disliked the whole idea of having to pretend to be engaged to someone else.

It was Lareen he would like to take with him to France, not the insignificant, unknown and, up till now, badly dressed Varia Milfield.

'Poor Mr. Blakewell,' Varia thought to herself.

After about ten minutes, he returned to the table, scowling and looking particularly unapproachable.

"I hope you won't mind, Miss Milfield," he said. "But my father particularly wishes to see you before I take you home. I thought, Madame René, we would drop you on the way. We don't want to keep you any longer. It has been a long day for you."

"That is kind of you," Madame René said. "But it is quite unnecessary for you to take me anywhere. I have a car parked in Berkeley Square."

They drove to Berkeley Square. Madame René got out of the Bentley and held out her hand to Varia.

"Bonsoir, ma petite," she said. "Enjoy yourself in France. Remember it is all a new experience."

"Thank you so very much for everything," Varia answered.

Madame René said goodnight to Ian and walked towards her car. Varia waved and they drove round the square down Davies Street and on towards Regent's Park.

They drew up at the big square portico of a great grey stone mansion. The butler showed them through a black and white marble Hall and into a fine panelled sitting-room. Sir Edward was sitting in front of the fire with a rug over his knees.

"Ah! Here you are!" he exclaimed. "Forgive me for not rising to greet you, but my leg has been exceedingly troublesome all day."

"Please don't move," Varia pleaded.

She put her hand into his and saw him looking at her hair.

"I don't know how to thank you for what you have done for me, Sir Edward. I feel I ought not to take all those lovely clothes."

"You couldn't go to France without them, could you now?" he asked with a twinkle in his eye.

Varia smiled back.

"Oh, no!" she replied. "They would think your son was making a pretty poor marriage if they saw me in my old clothes."

Sir Edward put back his head and laughed.

"So you have got a sense of humour as well as being pretty," he said. "I hope you have managed to make Ian laugh, too. He's been going about as dour as a Scot who has lost half-a-crown and found a threepenny bit."

Ian moved across the room to stand beside his father's chair.

It was true, Varia thought, that he ought to smile more. He was good-looking, with square-cut features, strong chin and determined mouth.

His grey eyes, too, deep set in his head, were intelligent and, she was sure, missed nothing of what was going on around him.

It was only his expression that was at fault — sulky, a little resentful, and all, she assumed, because of Lareen.

"Well, I've thought of something that has been forgotten," Sir Edward said. He was obviously enjoying every moment of seeing his plans fall into place like the pieces of a jigsaw puzzle. "Have you any idea what that could be, Ian?"

"No, I'm afraid not, Father," his son replied.

"Then I will tell you," Sir Edward said triumphantly. "You've forgotten the ring, my boy! Oh yes," he added as he saw the words of protest rising to his son's lips. "I know you're only supposed to be unofficially engaged, but that's no reason why Varia shouldn't wear a ring."

He smiled as if delighted to find he could find fault with his son.

"Oh, well, I see I have to think for you. I've had these sent over on approval. See what you think of them."

He picked up a large leather case which stood on the table beside him and snapped it open. There were six rings in it, sparkling against the black velvet with which it was lined, and to Varia's eyes they were all fabulous.

"Now, take the box," Sir Edward commanded, "and make up your minds between you which you are going to have."

He thrust it into his son's hands and Ian carried it to a table on which there stood a lamp and set it down directly under the light. Slowly Varia walked across to join him.

As she did so, the telephone rang at Sir Edward's elbow and he picked it up.

"Hello! Oh, it's you, Sampson, is it?" she heard him say. "I've been trying to get hold of you all day. Where the hell have you been? What's happening on the market?"

She reached Ian's side and stood looking down at the rings.

"Which do you want?" he asked.

Because of the abruptness in his tone she resisted an impulse to do things the easy way and choose the one she liked best.

"Which do you think the most suitable?" she asked politely.

"I haven't the slightest idea," he replied.

"Nor have I," she said. "I've never had to choose an engagement ring before."

His eyes met hers for a second and he realised that she was deliberately taunting him.

"Damn it all, nor have I," he answered almost savagely. "And I should have thought this was quite unnecessary."

"Your father apparently thinks otherwise."

"Can't you see the old devil's enjoying every moment of it?" Ian asked savagely.

There was no need to lower his voice for Sir Edward was bellowing into the telephone, apparently berating his stockbroker because some of his snares had gone down.

"I am sorry to be such a terrible nuisance to you," Varia said in mock humility.

"You're all right, you are getting something out of this," Ian said sharply.

There was something in his tone besides the roughness of his words which made Varia flinch. For a moment she thought of saying: "So are you, and there's no need to be rude." Then, with an effort she restrained herself.

Instead she said gently and sincerely:

"I'm sorry if you hate it so much. It won't last long. You'll find that a week passes very quickly."

Ian had the grace to look ashamed.

"I apologise," he said stiffly, and because she felt she had teased him a little unmercifully, Varia bent forward and took a ring from its velvet sheath.

It was an aquamarine, square-set and flanked on each side by baguette diamonds. She held it for him to see.

"I like this one best," she said. "Shall we have it?"

"You must have what you want," he replied.

Behind them Sir Edward put down the telephone with a little bang.

"Well, have you chosen one?" he barked.

Varia walked towards him with the ring in her hand.

"I think this is the prettiest," she said. "If

67

it fits me, it will do beautifully."

"Try it on then," Sir Edward commanded; but when she would have done so, he put out his hand to restrain her.

"No, no," he said. "Ian had better play his part. Might as well get used to it. Come on Ian, put the ring on Varia's finger in the prescribed manner."

Ian shot his father a look of fury and his lips tightened, but he took the ring from Varia and waited for her to hold out her left hand. She had a sudden reluctance to do so.

Just for a moment she thought, 'This pretence has gone far enough.'

The fact that a strange, rather churlish young man was standing there with a ring, waiting to put it on her engagement finger, seemed to break the dream that every girl cherishes at the back of her mind. The moment of her engagement.

An action of love to be followed by that magical moment in the wedding ceremony when another ring makes her a married woman.

She had an impulse to cry out, "No, no, I will put it on myself."

It was too late. While she had hesitated, Ian had captured her hand and was pressing the ring over the knuckle of her third finger.

She felt the strength of his fingers on hers;

she felt the sudden coldness of the ring; and then it was there, fitted into place, shining in the light — a lovely and expensive piece of jewellery that she had never in all her imaginings thought of possessing.

An engagement ring, and yet it was only a pretence one.

She did not know why, but she had a sudden feeling that the ring had trapped her. She wanted to run away. She wanted suddenly to call the whole thing off.

"No, I don't think it . . . fits," she said in a sudden panic. "I think I'll . . . try another . . . one."

She heard her own voice, breathless and yet on edge, as if it was the voice of a stranger. And then, surprisingly, she was answered, not by Sir Edward but by Ian.

"It fits perfectly," he said firmly. "That is the ring we will have."

Varia slept badly that night.

She lay awake in the darkness thinking of the events of the day and feeling miserable, rather than elated, by all that had happened.

She tried to think of the wonderful clothes she was to have, the adventure of going abroad. But, instead she could only see Pierre's dark eyes looking down into hers, and his voice saying "Promise me that you won't disappear again."

And when she was not thinking of Pierre she found herself remembering the disdain in Ian Blakewell's face. She could hear the icy cold of his voice and knew that he hated her!

Questions which she could not answer seemed to sit at the end of her bed and torture her.

What did she know about Pierre except that he was dark and attractive and wished to see her? Nothing! And yet her heart told her in the darkness that she wanted to know more.

'What would Mummy think of it all?' she asked herself.

Then at the very thought of her mother she felt a warm glow of happiness run through her which made all her other troubles and her miseries pale into insignificance.

Her mother was safe! Her mother was in Switzerland! Her mother had a chance of recovery!

"Thank you! Thank you, God!" Varia breathed softly and tried to ignore the little ache in her heart because, through her own stupidity, she had lost Pierre de Chalayat — perhaps for ever.

When morning came, she had a wild idea of hurrying into the Park in case he should

70

be waiting for her. But she knew he would not be likely to be there so early.

At eleven o'clock a taxi drew up at the door. She saw that there were several suitcases by the driver's seat and that inside a young woman was surrounded by cardboard boxes.

"I think you are looking for me," Varia said as she opened the door.

"Yes, Miss Milfield, I've brought your clothes," a gay voice answered.

Varia looked into a pair of twinkling hazel eyes and recognised Madame René's assistant.

"I'm June!" the girl announced. "Madame René couldn't get away from the shop but she sent her best wishes for a successful journey."

"There seem to be rather a lot of things," Varia said looking at the suitcases and boxes which the taxi driver was beginning to unload.

"Oh, I expect you will find when you get to France that you 'haven't a thing to wear,'" June announced with a smile, and the two girls looked at each other and laughed.

With the help of the driver they got everything upstairs.

June took a dress out of a cardboard box.

It was a soft shade of blue and was made of silk tussore. There was a coat of very fine tweed to match it in a deeper shade of blue.

"Is that what I am going to wear on the journey?" Varia asked. "It's very pretty."

"It's one of Mr. Myles' most successful models," June said. "I didn't think he would ever let it out of the Collection."

"Why has he?" Varia asked. "Why has he let me have all these clothes? It must be very inconvenient just now in the middle of the season."

June stared at her.

"Do you mean to say you don't know?"

"I've not the slightest idea."

"Well, it's because of Sir Edward Blakewell, of course," June explained. "He's behind Mr. Myles. I mean, he's put up the money for the shop and everything. When he wants something, naturally it has to be done."

"So that's why it is, is it?" Varia exclaimed. "I had no idea."

"Oh, yes! Sir Edward discovered Mr. Myles. He was struggling along in quite a small way. Then Sir Edward met him, saw some of his designs and set him up in Mayfair. His very first collection was a roaring success. The papers went mad over it."

"Sir Edward's clever, isn't he?" Varia said.

"I suppose he is," June agreed. "He's certainly very frightening. We're all terrified of him at the shop. And when we heard yesterday that he was sending someone to be dressed, we all wondered what she would be like."

"Were you surprised when you saw me?" Varia enquired.

"Well," June answered cautiously, "you weren't what we expected. You see, the only girls Sir Edward has dressed before have been models whom he has been sending out to South America or the south of France. You're different. But all the same I think it's a jolly good idea."

"What . . . what's a good idea?" Varia asked curiously.

"That you should show Lyons how an ordinary English lady dresses."

"Did Sir Edward tell you that was what I was going to do?" Varia asked.

"No, he didn't tell us, but Madame René did. It's true, isn't it?"

"Yes, yes . . . I suppose so," Varia answered, feeling the colour rise in her cheeks at having to lie.

As Varia started to put on the new clothes, June, sitting back on her heels on the floor, said:

"What do you think of young Mr. Blakewell?"

"What do you think of him?" Varia parried.

"I don't know," June said reflectively. "He used to come round the shop quite a lot when Lareen was with us. But somehow we never got to know him any better. The girls were furious because he was so stand-offish. But Lareen used to tell us he was shy."

"Shy!" Varia repeated the word in astonishment.

It was something she would never have connected with Ian Blakewell.

"That's what she told us," June said. "I must say I rather doubted it myself."

"I don't think he's shy, somehow," Varia said reflectively, then added: "I saw Lareen last night. She's very lovely, isn't she?"

"Very affected," June corrected.

"Do you like her?" Varia asked.

June shook her head.

"Not much," she said. "I don't hate her as Madame René does. But Lareen's not my favourite pin-up! She's difficult to work with — very temperamental and flies into a passion at the slightest thing."

Varia hesitated before she put the next question.

Then, not looking at June, she said:

74

"Is Mr. Blakewell in love with her?"

"I suppose so," June answered. "He was always coming to take her out, waiting for her outside in his car — that was until Sir Edward found out."

"What happened then?" Varia enquired.

"I hear that there was a dickens of a row," June answered. "Anyway, Lareen got the sack. She's working for one of our rivals now and, what's more, she's taken one or two of our best customers away. That hasn't exactly endeared her to Sir Edward or Madame René."

June suddenly jumped to her feet.

"That reminds me," she said. "I shall be out on my neck if I stay here too long. Madame René's instructions were that I was to help you to pack and dress and go straight back."

Before June had finished speaking, the telephone interrupted by shrilling noisily on the table beside the window.

Varia picked up the receiver.

"Is that you, Miss Milfield?" a voice asked.

"Yes," Varia replied. "Who is it?"

"Sir Edward's Butler, Miss. Sir Edward wishes to speak to you."

There were some clicks at the other end as if she was being put through to another room, and then she heard Sir Edward's deep, impatient voice saying:

"Is that you, Varia? Ian will be arriving for you at any moment. He left here some time ago."

"I'm ready," Varia said.

"Splendid! I'd hoped to come and see you off," Sir Edward said. "But my Doctor refuses to allow me to get up today. Ian has full instructions about everything, and you know what to do when you get there? Play your part convincingly. I'm relying on you, you know."

"I'll do my best," Varia promised.

"That's what I hope," Sir Edward approved. "I shall doubtless be telephoning you or Ian while you are there. Be cautious what you say on the telephone. So much depends on you, as you are well aware."

"I will be careful," Varia promised.

"Good-bye, my dear! And thank you for doing this."

Sir Edward did not wait for her response but put the receiver down.

"I must go," June said behind her. She had packed Varia's personal things which she had left ready in a suitcase and had now locked it and the hat box.

"It's been fun talking to you, Miss Milfield. When you come back, do let me know if the whole thing was a success. I expect you'll sell hundreds of dresses."

"I . . . I hope so," Varia said hesitantly.

At that moment the door bell pealed.

"That will be Mr. Blakewell!" Varia exclaimed.

"I'll skip then," June said. "Cheerio! Have a good time."

She picked up her handbag and ran down the stairs. Varia heard her open the front door and say in the demure, rather silky tones which she guessed was her shop voice:

"Good morning, Mr. Blakewell! Miss Milfield is quite ready."

She must have slipped past him because Varia then heard Ian Blakewell coming up the narrow stairs.

She stood indecisively in the middle of the room, feeling suddenly terribly embarrassed and not knowing quite what to say or what to do.

He reached the tiny landing and bent his head to enter the sitting-room door. He was bigger than she remembered, Varia thought; in fact, he seemed to fill the whole room with his tall, broad-shouldered presence.

"Good morning! I hear you are ready," he said awkwardly. "Is all this luggage yours?"

"It belongs to Mr. Myles, if that's what

you mean," Varia said with a smile.

"Good heavens! I can't imagine you'll want all that for just a short visit!"

"I think your father expects me to be a credit to the firm."

He didn't smile as she expected. Instead he just said rather disagreeably:

"Well, we shall certainly have to pay a lot of overweight on the plane."

Then he crossed the room to the window and opening it said to his chauffeur who was obviously waiting below:

"Will you come up and fetch the luggage, Bates?"

It took quite some time to pack the suitcases into the Bentley. Bates filled the boot, the front seat and all available space inside.

Varia had a quick look at herself in the mirror before she left the flat.

She wondered if Ian had noticed the difference between the vision in blue and the girl who had come trembling into the office only a few days ago, wondering why the boss should have sent for her.

But if he saw any change he made no remark on it.

They drove to London Airport almost in silence and only as they emerged from the tunnel did Varia begin to feel her heart beat quicker with the excitement of what lay ahead.

Nobody had asked her, so she had not mentioned the fact that she had never flown before. Nobody had asked, so she had told no-one that she had never been to France and, in fact, this would be her first visit to the Continent.

'Thank goodness I can speak French,' she thought, remembering the long, tiring lessons that she had endured with an old French woman in the village when she was a child.

"We've got plenty of time," Ian said as the car drew up at the entrance. "One's never quite certain with the traffic how long it is going to take."

"No, I suppose not," Varia said.

She wondered as she spoke whether all the conversation would be in this vein.

The weather; the traffic; everything that was commonplace and ordinary. All the things which her father used laughingly to describe as "bromides."

She stood beside Ian while the luggage was weighed before they moved to another desk where the tickets were inspected.

Then they went upstairs to where, in the long hall, people were congregating outside numbered entrances to the Customs Hall.

"We've got plenty of time," Ian repeated again, and they seated themselves on a leather-covered sofa.

They had hardly done so when Varia heard Ian give a startled exclamation. She looked quickly at him and saw that he was staring back the way they had come with a look of utmost astonishment on his face.

She followed the direction of his eyes and saw that advancing towards them, wearing a vivid emerald-coloured suit and being the cynosure of all eyes, was Lareen.

There was no doubt at all that she was looking particularly stunning, to judge by the expression on the faces of the men who turned to watch her pass.

No-one could help looking at her, Varia thought. She was not only beautiful, she was sensational.

For a moment it seemed as if Ian was paralysed by her sudden appearance, and then, as she reached them, he jumped to his feet.

"Lareen! What are you doing here?"

"What do you think?" she enquired. "I've come to say good-bye, which is something you have omitted from your itinerary."

"I tried to telephone you this morning, but the line was engaged," Ian said.

"What's this journey about?" Lareen asked querulously. "And who is this girl you

80

are taking with you?"

"I think you met Miss Milfield last night," Ian said, turning towards Varia.

Lareen ignored the hand that Varia instinctively put forward; her eyes flickered over her and there was a sudden hostility in her voice as she said:

"Dressed by Martin Myles! And you were with Madame René last night. What's the story behind it all? Or do I suspect an elopement?"

The last question was obviously meant to be a joke and Varia wondered whether Ian intended to tell her the truth.

"Now, listen, Lareen," he spluttered. "I'm going out to Lyons on a most important job for my father. Miss Milfield is accompanying me. She works in the main office. I have a contract to make — a very important contract that my father doesn't wish talked about."

"I still think you should have told me she was going with you," Lareen said pettishly. "And if I hadn't found you at the Berkeley last night, I don't believe you would ever have let me know you were going to France. Really, Ian! I think you are behaving in a very peculiar fashion."

"I was going to telephone you tonight," he said.

"So you say now," Lareen replied with a toss of the head. "But I see no reason why I should believe you."

"It's the truth," Ian said quietly. "I'm only going for a week, and entirely on business."

"Then why all this hole-in-the-corner manner of doing it? That's what I want to know," Lareen said looking at Varia again with a look of suspicion which she made no attempt to disguise.

Feeling embarrassed, Varia opened her bag as if she was searching for something in it.

As she did so, she saw the engagement ring in it and wondered mischievously what would happen if she put it on her finger and flaunted it.

As if taking a hint from Varia's action, Ian put his arm under Lareen's elbow and drew her to one side.

They were out of earshot, but Varia could see that they were obviously having a row. Lareen's eyes were beginning to flash and more than once she stamped her foot angrily.

"Will the passengers for Flight Four-Two-Three to Lyons please take their places in Channel Four?" came over the tannoy.

People began to move past Varia to the door where an air hostess, in her grey uniform, had appeared with a list in her hand.

Slowly Varia got to her feet, looking expectantly towards Ian.

He also had heard the announcement and turning his head moved a little away from Lareen. She followed him and now, once again, they were in earshot and Varia heard her say:

"There are so many things we must talk about. Wait until the next plane. Please, Ian."

She was almost pleading with him, yet Varia had the feeling that she was doing it only to exert her power over him. She wanted him to obey her, not so much because she wished to be with him, but to prove, perhaps to herself and certainly to him, that she could hold him.

"I am sorry, it's impossible! Quite impossible!" Ian said. "We've got to go now."

"But, Ian . . ." Lareen protested.

Almost abruptly Ian turned towards Varia.

"Are you ready?" he asked unnecessarily.

She was just about to reply when a small man came panting up to them. He was hatless and his too long hair was dishevelled as if by the wind.

"I say, Mr. Blakewell!" he gasped. "I thought I was going to miss you. I want a statement, if you please. And one from Miss Milfield."

"Hello, Davis!" Ian said coldly. "What do you want a statement about?"

"I've just been talking to Sir Edward," Mr. Davis replied, pulling a notebook and a pencil out of the pocket of his coat. "He tells me there's an engagement in the offing and that you're off to France to show your future wife to the biggest silk importers to this country. Quite a story! What have you got to say about it?"

"Your future wife! What the hell does he mean by that?" Lareen interposed, her voice shrill with astonishment.

The newspaper man seemed to realise for the first time that she was there.

"Hello, Beautiful!" he remarked familiarly. "I didn't notice you — which is unusual! Are you seeing off the happy pair or am I going to get a statement from you too?"

Lareen ignored him.

"What does this mean?" she asked Ian. And then her voice rose suddenly. "You dirty, underhand swine! So this is what you've been up to, is it? This is why I haven't seen you so much for the past few weeks."

"Lareen! Let me explain," Ian begged.

"I don't want any explanations from you," she stormed. "It's quite obvious what's happened. So your father has won, has he? He's got rid of me and now he's chosen a nice, mealy mouthed little puppet who'll do exactly what is expected of her. And if that is how you feel about it, you're welcome to her, and you can both go to hell!"

Lareen turned on her heel as she spoke and walked away. Ian made a gesture as if he would go after her, but once again the voice came over the air.

"Will the passengers for Flight Four-Two-Three come at once to Channel Four? I repeat! Will . . ."

"Here! What's going on?" Mr. Davis asked, a glint of excitement in his eyes as he sensed that there was a story here.

"Oh, go to the devil!" Ian ejaculated rudely.

He took Varia roughly by her arm as he spoke and hustled her away from the newspaper reporter towards the air hostess who was standing alone at the door into the Customs Hall.

"But, Mr. Blakewell! Mr. Blakewell!"

Varia could hear Mr. Davis's despairing cry following them and she realised that for the moment they had escaped his questioning.

At the same time, she knew by the frown between his eyes, the furious expression on his face, that Ian was very angry indeed.

It was not surprising, she thought, and wondered what had made Sir Edward give out such information, knowing that there was every chance of the reporter reaching them before their plane took off.

As she thought of it, she realised how implicated she, herself, was, and began to feel angry on her own account. Supposing her mother got to hear of it.

What would June and Madame René think when it appeared in the papers?

'It will make me look such a fool,' Varia thought to herself.

She looked up into Ian's scowling face and asked:

"Why has your father done this? I can't understand it."

"You would, if you knew my father," Ian replied unexpectedly.

"He said it was to be a secret. That was the whole idea."

"What he says and what he does are always quite different matters," Ian replied repressively. "But we can't discuss it here."

"Will the passengers for Flight Four-

Two-Three to Lyons come this way, please?"

The crisp clear tones of the air hostess galvanised everyone into action. They pushed through the door, followed her quickly along the corridor and down the covered steps to the aeroplane.

Ian showed Varia into a seat. She settled herself next to the window and glancing at him from behind her eyelashes, saw that he was still furiously angry. His lips were set in a tight tine, his eyes smouldering, a heavy frown creasing his forehead.

She tried to remember that she was angry too, but could think of nothing but that in a few moments they would be up in the air.

Now the aeroplane was moving down the runway. This was it, she thought. This was the moment when they would either rise or fail to do so.

Vividly to her mind came stories of aeroplanes that had turned over, crashed and burst into flames.

She felt suddenly sick with fear. She looked through the window and saw the ground rushing past. She wanted to cry out that she couldn't go; that she must stay behind because she had remembered something, anything, so long as they did not take off!

Then suddenly she felt a hand on hers.

"Are you quite all right?" Ian asked in what seemed to her a surprisingly kindly voice. "You are not frightened, are you?"

Almost involuntarily her fingers closed over his. She forgot everything except that he was strong, a man and that she could hold on to him.

"I am a little," she whispered. "You see, I've never been up in the air before."

"Poor child," he said. "I never imagined this was your first trip. It's quite all right, you know. Far safer than being in a motor car."

"I . . . I'm sure . . . it is," she stammered.

She knew that the warm security of his hand holding hers was something that could sustain her and take away her fears. Why, she did not know.

"It's quite all right," he said soothingly. "Look, we're up!"

She looked almost incredulously from the window. They were in the air and she hadn't realised it, rising, rising, the houses below them growing smaller and smaller.

She could see the roads with the cars tearing along, looking like toy cars that children played with. There were fields with their irregular outlines, a lake, a wood, all looking exactly like a child's models.

"We're up in the air!" she exclaimed incredulously.

"Yes, and quite safe," he answered.

She turned and smiled at him, still holding on to his hand.

"I never thought flying would be like this," she said.

"Like what?" he asked curiously.

She thought for a moment.

"Like being happy. Like being carried away with one's own thoughts," she said slowly, thinking it out. "Only this way one's body goes too."

"That's the nicest way of expressing it that I've ever heard."

It was the first time he had ever said anything pleasant to her and to her surprise she felt her eyes drop before his. She was suddenly conscious that she was still holding his hand.

She moved her fingers.

"I'm all right . . . now," she said a little tremulously. "Thank you for being . . . so kind to me."

"I ought to have thought of it before," he frowned. Her hand was free and she relaxed back against the cushions of her chair.

"Now I can say I have flown!" she said. "I've often felt ashamed of being so old-fashioned when other girls have talked about going places by aeroplane and I had never travelled in anything faster than a train."

"I shouldn't be ashamed of being old-fashioned," Ian said unexpectedly.

"Why?" she asked.

"Because it's rather wonderful to find someone who isn't up-to-date, who hasn't done everything and been everywhere. In fact, it's a welcome change."

"I'm glad you feel like that," Varia said. "Because I've another confession to make. I've never been abroad before."

"I somehow expected that," he said. "Is that also making you afraid?"

She considered for a moment and then she said:

"Not . . . if you . . . will be . . . kind to me. It's always rather frightening meeting a lot of . . . strange people one doesn't know. But . . . if you . . . will be . . . kind . . ."

Her voice trailed away into silence.

He looked at her and then he smiled.

"I promise to be kind," he said. "Will that make it better?"

Chapter Three

They arrived at the Lyons Airport about four o'clock.

As they swept down from the sky, circling lower and lower, towards the spires and towers of the churches and the red roofs of the houses, Varia had another moment of fright.

She saw two silver rivers, meeting, it seemed to her, in the centre of the town, and then, before she could see more, before she could really be conscious of her own fear of landing, there was a slight bump.

They had touched down and were taxiing down the broad concrete runway towards the white airport building in the distance.

"You see, we've arrived safely," Ian said.

As she turned her face towards him, she saw that he was smiling in an almost friendly fashion at her.

She thought to herself that he was

pleased, in some extraordinary way, at her weakness and for the moment at least, because he could patronise her, he was no longer fighting her.

"I expect Monsieur Duflot will be meeting us," Ian said as they walked in the sunshine towards the passport Control and from there into the Customs.

His supposition was right, for no sooner had they reached the Customs Shed than they saw at the far end of it a barrier with a crowd of people behind it. Amongst them was a short, stocky little man with grey hair who was waving effusively.

Ian acknowledged the greetings by raising his hat and forcing a somewhat stiff smile to his lips.

"Duflot is here," he said to Varia. "Personally, I've always found him a crashing bore, and I imagine that the rest of the family are the same."

Varia did not know what to reply to this. At the same time she was feeling grateful that for the moment at any rate, Ian had retracted his hostility and was at least treating her like a human being.

As they reached the barrier, Monsieur Duflot pushed everyone aside to rush forward with outstretched hands.

"*Mon cher* Ian! I am delighted to see

you!" he cried, shaking Ian's hand effusively and clapping him on the shoulder at the same time. "This is indeed a pleasure, and you have brought your charming *fiancée* with you! *Ma'm'selle, je suis enchanté!*"

He raised Varia's hand to his lips; then, talking nineteen to the dozen in a mixture of quite good English interspersed with interjections in French, he ushered them outside where a large car and a chauffeur in resplendent grey uniform were waiting.

"This is the first time I have been to France," she replied to one of his queries.

Monsieur Duflot clasped his hands together in ecstasy.

"What an occasion! And what a compliment to me and my family that the first night you should pass in our beautiful country will be under our poor roof. We are honoured, *Ma'm'selle.* We must make this a special celebration, yes?"

Varia glanced at Ian under her eyelashes and saw, as she half-expected, that he was scowling.

She was quite certain he was not going to look forward to any special celebrations which must take place because of his supposed *fiancée.*

Because she thought it would help, she answered deprecatingly:

"Oh, but Monsieur, I don't want to interfere with your business arrangements. It is so kind of you to let me come with . . . with . . . Ian, and I shall be perfectly happy to look round the town while you are working."

She realised, as she stumbled over Ian's name, that it was the first time she had either spoken of him or addressed him as anything but Mr. Blakewell.

"We are very proud of our city, *Ma'm'selle,*" Monsieur Duflot was saying. "Tomorrow we must take you to see the beauties of the Rhône and the Saône, and you must also visit the Musées and the Cathédrale."

"Perhaps Madame Duflot will show Miss . . . er . . . Varia around," Ian said hastily. "You and I have got a lot to discuss, Monsieur."

"Ah, but you must be careful!" Monsieur Duflot said with a roguish look in his eye. "If you neglect a pretty girl for too long, someone else will console her. That is true in every country, but most especially in France."

He laughed heartily at his own joke. Varia, feeling embarrassed because of what she knew Ian must be feeling, tried to turn the conversation by asking the name of

94

some building they were passing.

"That is the Hôtel de Ville," Monsieur Duflot explained. "And something you must certainly visit. It is very fine and it was built in the reign of Louis XIV."

There were several other buildings which he pointed out to her before, finally, they drew up at an imposing looking house in a quiet side street.

The chauffeur jumped out to ring the bell and almost instantly the door was opened by a manservant who hurried to help a boy carry in the luggage.

The house was large, but the rooms inside it were quite small. There seemed to be an enormous number of them through which they passed until they came to what was obviously the main sitting-room, where quite a number of the Duflot family were congregated.

It took Varia some time before she grasped that they were, indeed, all relations.

There was Madame Duflot and three children of varying ages, including a rather plain young girl who Varia realised was the marriageable daughter who should have been affianced to Ian. There was Madame Duflot's old father who was deaf and could not be expected to rise from his chair.

There was Monsieur Duflot's mother who, they informed Varia proudly, was getting on for ninety. There were aunts and cousins, mostly of the female sex, who Varia gradually understood were all living in the house.

"I expect *Ma'm'selle* would like to take off her hat and wash her hands," Madame Duflot said. "Jeanne, will you take Mademoiselle Milfield upstairs? You know where she is sleeping."

"Oui, Maman," Jeanne said, and turning to Varia said in almost perfect English: "Will you come with me? I expect you are tired. I find flying very tiring."

"How well you speak English," Varia said admiringly.

"I have learned it ever since I was a small child," Jeanne answered. "My father is fond of the English and he has always wanted me to . . . speak like an English person."

There was a little pause before the word "speak" and Varia guessed that almost automatically Jeanne had been about to say that her father had always wanted her to marry an Englishman.

She led her up the stairs to a small, rather over-furnished room on the second floor. There was a narrow four-poster hung with spotlessly clean muslin and a muslin petticoat attached to an old-fashioned dressing-table.

"What a nice room!" Varia said almost automatically.

"It looks over the garden and therefore it is quiet," Jeanne replied. "Actually it is my room, but Maman thought you would find it noisy in the guest room which happens to open onto the street."

"Oh, but you shouldn't have bothered to move," Varia exclaimed. "I am sorry to be such a nuisance!"

"It is no trouble," Jeanne replied. "We had expected Mr. Blakewell to come alone; but when we heard that he was bringing his *fiancée,* we were all very delighted. May I offer you my good wishes and hope that you will be very happy?"

There was something a little wistful in her tone and suddenly Varia felt ashamed. It was so unkind to pretend and lie to these people who were obviously kind-hearted and very sincere in their efforts to be hospitable.

At the same time, she could not help feeling that Ian would have been horrified at the idea of having to marry someone as dowdy as Jeanne Duflot.

She was, indeed, a complete contrast to Lareen. She was not made up for one thing, except for a very little pale lipstick on her thin lips.

Her face was so shiny that it almost seemed highly polished, and her rather sallow skin was accentuated by the lank darkness of her uncurled hair. She had no nail varnish and her clothes had obviously been chosen for utility rather than because of their decorativeness.

Vaguely at the back of her mind Varia remembered that a French *jeune fille* was not supposed to look attractive until after she was married — in fact it was considered fast and improper if she did so. But Varia thought, married or unmarried, it would be difficult to make Jeanne look chic!

As they were standing there, the servants began carrying in the luggage.

"What a lot of things you have brought," Jeanne said, and Varia sensed a note of envy in her voice.

"There does seem rather a lot," she answered apologetically. "But, of course, we didn't know what you would be doing."

"Oh, we are going to be very gay," Jeanne answered quickly, as if not to be would be some reflection on their hospitality. "There is a big dinner and dance tomorrow night which Papa is giving to many of the important industrialists in the city. You will go to that, and, of course, Maman. I do not know yet whether I have been invited."

"Oh, but of course you must come," Varia answered.

"I do not know," Jeanne said with a little shrug of her thin shoulders. "Papa had not made up his mind. You see, everyone has to be paired and if there are not enough un-attached young men I should be an odd one out."

"But that mustn't happen . . ." Varia began, only to be interrupted by Jeanne who went on:

"There is a luncheon party the next day with much the same people. All our friends are very anxious to see you. Papa has talked so much about Sir Edward Blakewell and . . . his son. And now, of course, you will be one of the Blakewell family, and therefore we shall feel that we are doing business with you as well as your husband."

"Yes, I suppose so," Varia said, feeling as if she was being dragged into a quicksand from which there was no escape.

"There is a bathroom just across the passage," Jeanne was saying. "Shall I leave you while you wash and come back for you in about two or three minutes?"

"That will be very nice, thank you," Varia said.

Jeanne went from the room and Varia crossed the passage to the bathroom where she washed her hands.

When she came back into her bedroom, Jeanne was waiting for her.

"As you are English, Maman has prepared five o'clock tea," she said. "We do not usually have tea but this is a very special occasion."

"That is very kind of you," Varia said.

She felt the one thing that she would really enjoy would be a cup of tea and something to eat.

She was hungry, but when she went down to the sitting-room she found everyone seated formally round a table on which reposed one plate of rather dull-looking biscuits and a large silver tray containing the tea things.

The tea itself, however, was delicious, although no milk was provided, only slices of lemon.

"You must tell us about your journey," Madame Duflot said, and to Varia's embarrassment she found that when she spoke all the assembled company ceased talking and listened to her in complete silence.

It was most disconcerting and Varia found the most commonplace description of their flight drying up on her lips.

"It was the first time Miss . . . Varia had ever been up in an aeroplane," Ian said, stumbling, as usual, over the Christian name.

"Well, it will certainly not be the last," Monsieur Duflot said. "When you are married, you must come here very often with your husband. We could make business relations very much more entertaining if the wives accompanied their husbands."

"Thank you," Varia answered with a smile. "But I do not think my . . . my future husband will agree with you. He much prefers to travel without female encumbrances."

She knew she was being mischievous as she spoke, and she looked at Ian with laughter in her eyes and a smile on her lips.

"That is right," Ian said a little heavily. "I think business is conducted in a far more reasonable atmosphere without the inclusion of feminine distractions."

"Ah, but you are wrong . . ." Monsieur Duflot began.

As he was speaking a servant entered the room and spoke to Madame Duflot.

"What is that?" she asked.

The servant repeated what he had said and Madame turned towards Varia.

"I think you are wanted on the telephone,

Ma'm'selle," she said.

"But that is impossible," Varia protested. "No-one would ring me up here."

"It might be my father," Ian said, breaking off his conversation with Monsieur Duflot who was warming to his theme.

"Yes, of course," Varia said. "But I expect he will want to talk to you. Hadn't you better come too?"

"I will follow you in a moment," Ian said.

She guessed from his tone that he would want to speak to his father in private, doubtless to say what he thought about the statement which had been made to the Press.

So, feeling rather as if she was an advance guard to draw the fire of the enemy, Varia followed the manservant down the passage and into another room where the telephone stood on a desk facing the window.

It was a stiff, rather austere room which was obviously used as an office. As the servant shut the door behind him Varia picked up the receiver.

"Hello!"

"Mademoiselle Milfield?" a French voice enquired.

"I am speaking," she said, wondering if this was a preliminary to putting her through to Sir Edward.

"Varia! Is that you?"

For a moment she thought she could not have heard right, and then, in a low voice because she knew the answer, she asked:

"Who is it?"

"It is Pierre! Are you surprised to hear me?"

"How did you find out where I was?"

"I found out because I was desperate! Why did you not come last night?"

"I couldn't! It was quite impossible!" Varia said.

"Then why did you not talk to me? Why did you not tell me where I could find you?"

"It was impossible," she said again. "I was sorry, terribly sorry, but there was nothing else I could do but just send you a message."

"I am very angry with you, do you hear? Very angry indeed. When can I see you?"

"See you!" Varia repeated. "But I am in France — you are speaking to me at Lyons."

"I know that," came the answer, "because I am here too. I came in my own aeroplane."

"Your own aeroplane!"

"Yes, I happen to have one. Are you surprised?"

"Very surprised," Varia answered. "But I still don't understand how you found out where I was."

"Well, I will tell you. I went to your office."

"You didn't!" Varia exclaimed.

"Yes, I did. You see, when you left me in the Park yesterday, I was half afraid that I should never find you again. So I noted just which door in the street you went into after you ran away from me. Later I strolled up to have a look at it. I found it was the offices of 'Blakewell and Company.' Well, I happen to know quite a lot about Sir Edward Blakewell — and his son."

There was a little pause.

"Did you hear what I said, Varia?" Pierre asked.

"Yes."

"I said — and his son."

"I heard you," Varia answered.

"Well, now, I think you have got a little explaining to do. What are you doing with Mr. Ian Blakewell in Lyons?"

"I wonder you didn't find that out too," Varia said quickly.

"Oh, I found out a great deal!" Pierre said, with that little hint of laughter in his voice which she found almost irresistible. "I found out that Mr. Ian Blakewell was leaving for France and that Miss Milfield hadn't been to the office since the beginning of the week. In fact, everybody thought she had been sacked, although they were not certain of that."

"Who did you talk to?" Varia asked.

"Well, amongst other people a rather pretty girl called Sarah. She gave me your address!"

"I can't think how you managed to do all this," Varia said.

"I can do anything when I set my mind to it," Pierre answered. "But when I rang Sir Edward, he was most evasive."

"You rang Sir Edward?"

"Yes, why not?" Pierre demanded. "I know all about him. You see, I happen to live near Lyons."

"It doesn't seem . . . possible!" Varia cried.

"I know that coincidence is a very extraordinary thing — or should I say Fate? Do you believe in Fate, little Varia?"

"I don't know," Varia replied quickly. "What did Sir Edward say when you spoke to him?"

"I told him I was looking for a friend of mine whom I had promised to visit in London. He said that he thought Miss Milfield had gone to the country. That was when I put two and two together and guessed — because I knew that you were already going to France — that your escort would be the inestimable Mr. Ian Blakewell."

"I can't stay here talking," Varia said. "And I can't explain anything. It's . . . it's too . . . difficult."

"I want to see you," Pierre said. "Where will you meet me?"

"But I can't see you! Of course I can't!" Varia said. "I am here as a guest; every moment is planned!"

"Then I shall come and ring the front door and demand to see you," Pierre answered. "Shall I say I am a relation of yours? Or an old friend of the family?"

"You mustn't say anything of the sort," Varia retorted. "Please go away."

"I couldn't do that. It would be cheating Fate that brought us together," Pierre said. "When will you meet me?"

"I can't possibly say."

"I can. You must slip out tonight after dinner. I will be waiting for you at the bottom of the street. Turn right when you come out of the front door."

"How can I do anything of the sort?" Varia questioned.

"Oh, I know French households. If you're not going to a party, you will be tucked into bed at ten o'clock. Give the servant five hundred francs and tell him that you have got to go for a walk; it's an English habit that you can't break but you don't want to upset the household."

"I can't — of course, I can't!" Varia protested. "Besides I haven't got five hundred francs."

"It's quite easy," Pierre said soothingly. "Just trust me and know that I shall be waiting for you. And Varia, my sweet, adorable Varia, don't make me wait in vain."

"I can't do it, you know I can't," Varia said again. Even as she spoke she heard a sound outside the door. "I must go," she said quickly, and put down the receiver.

She turned just as the door opened and Ian came in.

"Was that my father?" he asked.

"I'm not certain," Varia replied quickly. "It . . . it was a very bad line with lots of interruptions. N . . . now they say they will ring back . . . 1 . . . later."

She knew as she spoke she was lying badly and looked guilty. She never had been able to be convincing in telling a falsehood and she thought, although she was looking away from him, that Ian appeared suspicious.

"I should have thought it was rather early for my father to ring up. Are you quite sure it was he?"

"I . . . I don't really know," Varia answered quickly. "I . . . just held . . . on."

"How annoying," he said. "Besides I wished to speak to him, but I suppose what I have got to say can keep."

"If he does come through again, will you ask him if there is anything in the evening papers?" Varia asked.

Ian crossed the room to stub out his cigarette in an ashtray.

"Will you be very annoyed if there is?"

"Yes, very," Varia answered. "I don't want my mother to hear . . . what . . . I am doing. Besides, she's never even heard me speak of you."

She hesitated a moment and then added:

"That's not true. I suppose I have mentioned you as being part of the office."

"Is that how you think of me?" Ian enquired. "It makes me sound like a desk or a chair, or something."

"How else would you expect me to think of you?" Varia asked. "You'd never spoken to me. You'd never even said good morning when we've passed in the passage."

"Didn't I do that?" he enquired.

"No, of course you didn't," Varia said. "We all thought it was disagreeable and rather stuck-up of you. There used to be arguments as to whether your thoughts were so far away that you didn't see us or whether you were deliberately rude."

Ian stubbed out his cigarette into an ash-tray.

"You make me sound intolerable," he said.

"I think we thought you were," Varia said cheerfully.

She expected to make him angry at her impertinence, but instead he laughed.

"At any rate you're frank."

"Why not?" she replied recklessly. "After all, when this week is over we never need see each other again."

"No, there's certainly that about it," he answered.

He looked at her, almost as if he was seeing her for the first time. Varia did not know why, but it gave her a strange feeling.

It was something she couldn't explain because it was like nothing she had ever felt before. It was ridiculous, but she felt a little breathless.

Then his eyes went towards the telephone. A sudden idea struck her.

"Why don't you ring her?" she asked.

"Ring whom?" he enquired.

"Lareen."

She saw him stiffen and realised that she had gone too far.

"I think you can leave my private affairs to me," he said coldly. "They are certainly no concern of yours."

"I'm sorry," Varia answered. "I was only trying to be helpful. Shall we go back to the sitting-room?"

"I think that would be best," Ian said frigidly.

He opened the door for her and she swept through it, her little chin held high.

'It's no use trying to be friends with him,' she told herself as she went down the passage. 'He's intolerable and nothing I can say or do will make him anything but an unpleasant young man.'

She could not help being amused in the next half-an-hour to notice how uncomfortable Ian was, sitting on a hard chair in the centre of the Duflot family and being made to answer questions which were not only formal in the extreme but excruciatingly commonplace.

She took her revenge on him by looking shy and referring nearly every question when it was addressed directly to her back to Ian.

"I really don't know," she would say demurely. "What do you think, Ian?" Or else, more mischievous still, she would say: "I know Ian would love to tell you about that."

She received one glance of hatred from him which made her giggle and after that

110

she didn't dare look at him.

"Dinner will be at seven-thirty," Madame Duflot suddenly announced, as the hands of the clock pointed to a quarter-to. "I expect you would like to go upstairs and change, would you not, *Ma'm'selle?*"

"Yes, please," Varia answered with relief.

Once again Jeanne took her up to the second floor and left her in the little bedroom, where she saw that everything had been unpacked.

She had just begun to take off her dress when there came a knock at the door.

"Entrez," she said, and a rather pretty maid, whom she had seen helping with the luggage, came in and closed the door behind her.

She had something under her apron. As she crossed the room, she drew out her hand and Varia saw that in it was a letter.

"Pour vous, Ma'm'selle."

"For me?" Varia questioned in surprise. Then she guessed who it was from.

"The gentleman said I was to give it to you when no-one was looking," the maid said in French in a low voice. "He also told me that you would wish to go out this evening — for a walk."

For one moment Varia contemplated saying, no. Then some little voice at the

111

back of her mind asked, 'why not?' Pierre had made everything easy for her.

He had obviously bribed the maid, had sent her a note which no-one would know about and he would have made sure that if she would go out with him, she would be able to get into the house again.

"Merci beaucoup," she said taking the letter in her hand. *"Vous êtes très gentille."*

The maid went from the room and Varia tore open the letter. Inside there were only a few words written on a sheet of crested paper.

I shall be waiting tonight — and always. Pierre.

Varia read it several times and then gave a little laugh of excitement. She couldn't believe this was really happening to her.

Two adventures running side by side — one rather pompous and frightening; the other equally frightening, but gay, light-hearted, amusing. And she thought, with a sudden heartbeat — perhaps something else.

She stood for a moment in the centre of the room, holding Pierre's letter in her hand.

'I shall go!' she told her conscience. 'Why shouldn't I?'

Varia crept slowly down the stairs, holding her breath every time the wood creaked. Her feet seemed to her, in her nervousness, to make a resounding noise on the polished steps.

She had almost decided not to go — wanting to meet Pierre yet half-afraid to commit herself to an adventure which she knew in her heart of hearts was wrong.

When she had gone up to bed, she had not undressed immediately. Instead, she had walked about her bedroom, undecided, arguing with her conscience.

'I mustn't go! I mustn't,' she told herself and longed to know if Pierre really was waiting for her.

She felt as if the dinner with the Duflot family had gone on for hours. Twelve people had sat down round the table and yet it seemed to her the only one who spoke was Monsieur Duflot.

He held forth at great length, ostensibly giving them all a lecture on the silk business and his own company's pre-eminence in their manufacturing, but, actually, as Varia well knew, trying to impress Ian.

She knew by the dullness in his eyes and the sharp line of his lips that Ian was bored. But he made a pretence of listening, even occasionally interjecting a remark or asking a question which showed that he was following what Monsieur Duflot was saying.

After dinner, stuffed with food and warmed by the delicious wine that had been served with the meal, they sat around the sitting-room, still listening to Monsieur Duflot.

"Tomorrow," he said, "if there is time, I must take this young lady to see our factory."

"I should like that very much," Varia said politely, feeling it was expected of her.

"She must also see the town," Madame Duflot interposed.

"But of course," her husband replied. "And, what is more, our citizens must see her. Sir Edward told me in his letter that many of the dresses *Ma'm'selle* will be wearing are made with our very own special silks."

"We are longing to see your clothes," Jeanne said with what Varia thought was a pathetic touch of envy in her voice.

"They are particularly pretty this season," she said.

"I cannot think how the young girls of today can afford many clothes at the high price they are — in France at any rate," Madame Duflot said a little tartly.

She looked almost accusingly at Varia who felt both ashamed and a hypocrite. Did they imagine that she was an heiress? she wondered, that she could afford such expensive things.

She knew, uncomfortably, that the dress she was wearing at dinner must have cost nearly one hundred pounds to the ordinary customer.

It was of pale aquamarine satin cleverly embroidered with sequins and tiny diamanté. It was short with a very tight bodice and a very full skirt, and Varia had stared incredulously at her reflection in the mirror before she had come downstairs.

Was this really the rather crushed little secretary who had gone to work morning after morning in Blakewell and Company's offices?

She looked at herself and could not help the sudden joy of knowing Pierre would see her like this.

If he had thought her attractive in her old grey suit, what would he think when he saw her now, with her hair beautifully done and the cleverly cut lines of the dress framing her figure to show the soft curves of her breasts and the tiny circumference of her waist?

She found it hard to listen to anything

that was being said. It was an effort to answer questions or to bring her attention back to the envious glances of Jeanne and the vaguely felt hostility of Madame Duflot.

She was thankful when Madame rose and said it was time for bed.

"You have a long day in front of you to-morrow," she said. "And I expect you will be late at the party which is to be given in the evening. I hope you will find everything you want in your room."

Varia thanked her and said good night politely to everyone in turn. When she reached Ian, she hesitated a moment and held out her hand. Monsieur Duflot let out a hearty laugh.

"You two young people mustn't be shy in front of us," he said. "You must look on Maman and me as the family. Kiss each other good night; you know you are both wanting to do so."

Varia felt herself flush, the colour rising vividly in her cheeks. But Ian, apparently quite imperturbable, bent forward.

For a moment she felt his lips against her flushed skin, and then, without looking at him, she turned away and let Jeanne lead her upstairs to her room.

There the dour battle of desire versus conscience began, only to be ended as there

116

came a little knock at the door.

"Who is it?" she asked, thinking it must be Jeanne and wondering what she would think to see her not undressed.

The door opened and the chambermaid stood there.

"It is safe now, *Ma'm'selle*," she whispered.

Varia stared at her. Should she refuse or should she take the path that had suddenly been made easy for her?

She looked at the maid for a moment with wide eyes and then, going to a drawer, drew out a soft wrap. It was of velvet in the same shade of blue and lined with white swansdown.

She wrapped it round her and without a word followed the maid from the room, switching out the light as she went. They moved slowly down the corridor. Varia knew that Ian slept a few doors away and every step seemed fraught with danger.

They reached the top of the stairs and began to descend slowly. There was the tick of a grandfather clock in the hall, the smell of the beeswax and cleanliness that was indescribable.

At last she had reached the bottom step to stand for a moment listening.

There was only silence except for the clock.

117

The little maid beckoned and Varia followed her past the big front door and down a passage to where, far less imposing, another door opened onto the street.

"I do not know what time you will be back, *Ma'm'selle,*" the maid said, "but here is the key. When you let yourself in, put it on the table just inside the door. I will be down early, before anyone else is awake, to put the chains on the door again and to take away the key."

"Merci beaucoup," Varia said.

She felt the key, cold in her hand, and realised that in her hurry she had forgotten to bring a bag. There was no time to worry about that. The door was open and she slipped through it into the street.

She felt suddenly afraid that the whole thing had been a hoax and Pierre had not meant her to come at all. Then, obedient to his instructions, she turned right and started to walk down the street.

It was then she saw him. He was waiting at the corner, but before she could reach him he had moved towards her holding out his arms.

"You have come!" he exclaimed. "You angel! You adorable, enchanting angel! I knew you would not fail me."

He raised her hands to his lips and kissed

them passionately, first one and then the other.

Then, as Varia made a little movement, he freed her instantly and putting his hand under her arm hurried her towards his car.

It was a magnificent Mercedes and he helped Varia into the front seat, covering her legs with a soft rug.

"Are you warm enough?" he asked, and there was a caress in his voice.

"I . . . I mustn't stay long," said Varia nervously.

He smiled at that, shut the door and walked round the car to get into the driver's seat. Without a word he started up the engine and began to drive through the town.

"Where are we going?" Varia asked.

"I want to show you my château," he said. "It is only fifteen miles outside Lyons."

"Oh, but I can't go there," Varia said quickly.

She did not know why, but she suddenly felt afraid. It was unconventional enough to meet Pierre; but to go to his house in the middle of the night was, she felt, definitely something that was socially wrong and which, therefore, she must refuse.

He turned to smile at her.

"So respectable! So strait-laced!" he teased. "Are you really like that or is it already the influence of the Duflot family?"

"It's me," she answered ungrammatically. "I . . . I don't think my mother would like me to go to a man's house at this hour. Besides, what would your family think?"

"I have no family," he answered. "Or, rather, none who are with me at the château. You do not suppose I would bore you with my relations, do you?"

Thinking of the Duflots, Varia could not help feeling relieved.

"All the same, I think it's too late," she said.

"Very well," he replied with an ease which somehow disarmed her. "We will only look at it from the outside. You need not get out, but I hope I will make you curious enough to want to see it tomorrow or the next day."

"But how can I?" she exclaimed. "You don't understand. Every moment is going to be filled up with receptions and parties."

"Then if it's really as bad as you make out, we shall have to meet at night!" Pierre said. "I expect we shall find a way."

"I mustn't do this again," Varia said, speaking more to herself than to him. "It's too dangerous. It's not fair to Sir Edward."

She spoke almost without thinking.

"You mean," Pierre said, "that Sir Edward has bought your free time as well as engaging you to show off his merchandise?"

"What do you know about it?"

"What I have guessed," Pierre grinned. "I know, you see, that there is a Silk Convention on at the moment. I know what Sir Edward's interests are, and also François Duflot's. I see that you are dressed up to the nines . . ."

He stopped, then said in a very different tone: "I haven't told you yet how lovely you are! I want to look at you — at your eyes, at your hair, and that ridiculously inviting mouth of yours. Have you any idea how provocative it is?"

"Provocative?"

Varia looked puzzled.

"It provokes me to want to kiss you," Pierre said. "But I think I am rather frightened of you, you are so very . . . respectable."

Varia tried to laugh lightly, but somehow it was difficult. She felt, instead, a glow of warmth creeping over her. She could feel her breath coming quickly between her lips. She felt excited with a strange, rather dangerous excitement.

"Now the town is left behind," Pierre said as they came into the open country.

It was all exquisitely beautiful in the

moonlight — the undulating road, the distant hills, the river on one side of them, a silver ribbon winding between high banks with occasional lofty crags.

But Varia found it difficult to think of anything but Pierre.

"How could you try and leave me behind," he was asking. "It was cruel and unkind of you, knowing how you had already made me suffer the first time I lost you."

"I think you are making it all up," she said, flirting for the first time in her life.

"Do you really think that?" he replied. "I wish I could tell you what I went through, wondering where you were, wondering how I could find you. You haunt me whatever I am doing. I even dream about you every night."

"What rubbish!" she answered, but the words were little more than a whisper.

Pierre was driving at a tremendous speed along the almost empty road.

Suddenly they turned through big, ornamental gates to drive down a long avenue of lime trees. At the far end of it there was a large grey château, exquisitely beautiful as it stood surrounded by dark trees, like a jewel framed in a velvet setting.

"Oh, my darling! *Ma petite!*" Pierre exclaimed. "You are so young, so exquisitely untouched. I think I realised that the very first moment I set eyes on you. Tell me, am I the first man in your life?"

"I don't know what you mean by that?" Varia said a little uncomfortably.

"I think you do," he answered. "Have many men made love to you? Have you ever loved any of them in return?"

This, at least, Varia could answer honestly. She shook her head.

"I knew it!" Pierre said triumphantly. "I was sure of it. You are like an English snowdrop; you are like a little white rose when it first comes into bud. *Chérie, Chérie,* I love you so much!"

He looked down into Varia's eyes and she felt herself held spellbound. Then, as he would have kissed her, bending his head with a practised grace, she turned her face away so that his lips found, not her mouth but her cheek.

"I love you!" he repeated, and now his arm went round her, drawing her close. "*Je t'adore!* Please, my own Varia, love me a little in return."

He was drawing her still closer to him, and then suddenly her hands came out to push him away.

"No! No!" she said in a frightened little

123

voice "It is too soon. I don't know you. Oh please . . ."

He was suddenly still, even though his lips were very close to hers.

"Why are you afraid?" he asked.

"I don't know," Varia answered. "But I am. Please, please take me back."

She was conscious, as she spoke, of the conflict within him. She knew it was quite easy for him to crush her resistance. She was so small and fragile and she knew by the strength of his arms that he was a very strong man.

Pierre brought the car to a standstill just in front of the house.

"It's lovely!" Varia exclaimed.

"I want you to think so," he answered. "It's my favourite house."

"Have you another one?" she enquired.

"Two or three more," he answered. "But this is the one I prefer when I have to live in the country."

"You must be very rich!" Varia ejaculated.

"Have you ever known a land-owner admit he's anything but starving?" Pierre retorted.

Then turning round in the seat to face her, with his arm running behind her head, he said:

"I don't want to talk about myself. I want to talk about you."

"That's very dull," she pouted.

"Not to me," he answered in his deep voice. "I can think of no more exciting subject. Tell me about yourself."

"It's just an ordinary story," Varia parried, feeling, in a kind of panic, that she mustn't tell him too much.

At the back of her mind she wondered how she could keep him from knowing of the pretence that she was playing with Ian to deceive the Duflots.

If there had been anything about them in the evening papers, she calculated that Pierre would have left London before they were out.

There was always the chance, of course, that it would be repeated in the morning papers. But even if it was, there was no reason why Pierre should see it here in Lyons.

And yet, if he did, she wondered what she should say. Could she bear to lie to him? To let him think that she was engaged to Ian?

And yet, whatever happened she must not break her vow to Sir Edward. That was one thing that in honour she could never do.

She knew, too, that when the moment came she would not put up much resistance. She wanted him to kiss her and yet, at the same time, she was afraid.

"Do you mean this? Do you really mean you want to go back?" Pierre's voice was deep and raw with emotion.

Just for one moment she hesitated, hating to hurt him and yet conscious of her own instinct which told her she must not surrender.

"Please," she pleaded.

"And if I let you go," he said. "If I do as you ask, will you promise me that you will come again? That I may show you the château? That I may drive you here, or anywhere else, so long as we are together?"

She raised her eyes to his, knowing that the moment of danger was past, but that she must not play with fire.

"I . . . promise," she said.

"Then I will do as you ask," he said. "I will do it because I want you to trust me. Once again, little bird, you have eluded me. Perhaps, though, I am the fool to let you go! Mayn't I kiss you just once?"

Instantly she turned her head.

"I don't know you well enough," she said.

"La première fois!" he said softly. "Well you must be allowed to choose your moment. But, oh, Varia! Don't keep me waiting for long."

He gave a little sigh and moved a little further away from her.

"You drive me to madness," he said. "I don't suppose any other man would draw back when he had gone so far. You say that you are afraid of me. Perhaps I, too, am afraid of you — afraid of hurting what is so beautiful, so perfect in its purity."

Varia put her hands up to her burning cheeks.

"I wish you wouldn't say things like that," she said. "It makes me feel so shy."

"But they are true, nevertheless," Pierre answered. "And why should I not tell you the truth? And tell you, too, again and again, that I love you?"

"I don't think love comes as quickly as that," Varia said.

"And what do you know about love?" he asked.

She knew it was a clever question because, indeed, she knew nothing.

'Could this be love?' she asked herself. With someone of whom she knew nothing, whom she had only met twice in her life before? She could not understand her own reluctance to let him kiss her, except a kind of inner fastidiousness and a fear of the unknown.

Because she had never been kissed, she

shrank from starting in this clandestine manner, doing what she knew was wrong because she ought not to have come in the first place.

"We must go back," she repeated.

"You are like the Snow Maiden whom no man could thaw," he said. "And yet, shall I promise you one thing, Varia?"

"What is that?" she asked.

"One day I will make you melt for me. I will make you understand passion and all that it means. I will teach you to love me as I love you. And then you will realise what life is really like — not just the schoolgirl's dream you are dreaming now."

There was a vibrant note of passion in his voice that made her instinctively move a little further away from him.

"I must go home," she repeated almost blindly.

He was silent for a moment and then he asked, almost humbly:

"You do love me a little, don't you, Varia?"

"I . . . think so," Varia whispered.

"Oh, my sweet, thank you for that," he said. "It is a crumb to a starving man, but nevertheless, a crumb."

He picked up her hand as he spoke and put it to his lips. He kissed the back of it and then the thumb and her fingers, one by one, and then he turned it over and kissed the palm.

She felt a sudden tremor pass through her and it frightened her, as the thought of a kiss had frightened her a little while earlier. She pulled her hands away from him.

"Let us go back," she said quietly. "It was wrong of me to come, but it will make it worse if I stay very much longer."

He gave a little sigh that she felt was almost one of exasperation.

Then, without a word, he started up the car and turned it slowly round in front of the house.

They travelled at a tremendous speed in silence and only as they reached the centre of the town and started winding their way through the residential streets towards Monsieur Duflot's house did Pierre say:

"Will you think of me tonight? And remember that I did what you asked against every inclination to keep you and never let you go?"

"Thank you for bringing me back," she said.

"That isn't what I asked you," he replied. "I want you to think about me. I want you to realise how you have made me suffer. I shall not go to bed tonight. I shall walk about thinking of you, wanting you and burning for you. Does that mean anything?"

Varia put out her hand impulsively and laid it on his arm.

"Don't love me too much," she said.

"Why do you say that?" he enquired.

"Because I . . . I don't think I understand it," Varia said, striving to put her thoughts into words. "You are making it so big, such a . . . tremendous thing."

"That's exactly what it is," Pierre answered. "Tremendous, because I want you, because I love you, because you drive me crazy with your little nun's face and your mouth which promises very earthly delights."

He drew the car to a standstill and she saw that they were at the end of the street where she had met him.

He bent forward and kissed the top of her shoulder where the wide neck of the dress was scooped away to reveal the whiteness of her neck.

She felt his lips were burning her and then, before she could protest or cry out against his kiss, he had opened the door, jumped from the car and was hurrying round to open the door on her side.

His fingers held hers very tightly as he helped her on to the pavement.

"I shall telephone you tomorrow to find out what are your plans," he said. "I have got to see you, you know that."

"It may be difficult," she answered.

"I will see that maidservant again," he said. "She will need more bribery, but if necessary I will bribe the whole damned house. I am not going to let you escape me, Varia, however hard you try."

She looked up at him in the moonlight, thinking how handsome he was, and suddenly her eyes were soft.

"I don't . . . think I want to . . . escape," she whispered, and then before he could reply she was running away from him down the street, hurrying towards the small door to which she had the key.

There was no-one about, she noted with relief; and when finally she reached the Duflots' house and looked back, Pierre also had disappeared. She heard him start up the car, then she inserted the key in the lock and turned it.

She had reached the hall and was just about to raise her foot on to the first step of the stairs when a door opened and a shaft of yellow light came flooding out into the hall. She started, feeling her fear of being discovered stab through her almost like a physical pain.

Then she saw whose broad shoulders filled the open doorway.

It was Ian who stood there. Ian, wearing a silk dressing gown over his evening trousers.

For a moment Varia felt paralysed. She could only stand like a statue staring at him, her eyes wide, very dark and frightened in the whiteness of her face.

"Where have you been?"

Ian's question was spoken in a low voice — so low that it seemed almost beneath his breath — and yet she heard it. She did not answer and after a moment he said:

"Come in here. We don't want to waken everyone."

With an effort, feeling almost as if her feet were weighted with lead, Varia crossed the hall, passed him and entered the room.

Ian shut the door and turned to face her.

"Where have you been?" he repeated. "I happened to open the window because my room was hot. I looked out and saw you disappearing round the corner of the street." He paused a moment and added: "You were not alone."

Varia took a deep breath.

"I went out to meet a . . . friend," she said.

"A friend in Lyons?" he asked almost sarcastically.

"Yes, a friend in Lyons," she repeated.

"He telephoned me tonight — when you thought that your — father was trying to get through. It was stupid of me not to tell you then."

"Are you in love with him?"

Varia's chin went up.

"I don't think you have any right to question me with regard to my private life," she answered.

"You have no private life at the moment," he snapped. "You are here to do a job. What you have done tonight might have jeopardised everything."

Varia twisted her fingers together nervously.

"I know that," she answered. "It was wrong of me to go out and I am sorry. I won't do it again."

She felt, rather than saw, that Ian's face did not relax its sternness.

"How can I trust you?" he asked.

"I have given you my word," Varia replied proudly. "I have said I will not go out at night again — not, at any rate, without letting you know."

Ian's attitude of stern disapproval suddenly seemed to relax.

"God knows," he said angrily, "I didn't want to put on this absurd act. But now that we have become involved, we must behave decently. We can't allow the Duflots to suspect either that they have been deceived or that my future wife, as they believe, has very peculiar morals."

His voice was deliberately insulting. Varia felt the blood rush in a crimson flood from her chin to her forehead.

"I've said I am sorry," she answered in a low voice. "Can't we leave it at that?"

"How can I really believe that you won't do it again? That you have not got some arrangement concocted to go for a meeting tomorrow?"

"He has asked to see me," Varia said, "but I told him that I thought it would be impossible."

"It is absolutely impossible; is that understood?"

He had come near to her as he spoke and now it seemed to her he was standing over her, bullying her. She felt frail and defenceless and suddenly very wretched.

She knew he despised her, knew he suspected far worse than what had actually occurred. But there was nothing she could say, nothing she could do. She looked up at him with her eyes half blinded with tears.

"I am . . . sorry. Please . . . can I go to . . . bed?"

As she spoke the tears overflowed and ran

down her cheeks. Large as dewdrops on a rose petal, they glittered in the light of the lamps.

"Dammit all, I don't want to be unpleasant . . ." Ian began.

But she turned away from him, moving quickly across the room to fumble for the handle of the door.

"Varia!" he said, and now there was almost a note of pleading in his voice.

But she did not wait. She opened the door and running across the hall, reached the stairs. She climbed them swiftly, regardless of any noise she might make, and then running down the passage, she opened the door of her own room and closed it behind her.

Only then did she release the control on herself and feel a tempest of emotion shake her.

Crying bitterly, she groped her way across the room and flung herself down on the bed.

She did not know why she was so unhappy.

She only felt as if her whole world was dark and empty; that she was alone as she had never been alone before.

Chapter Four

Varia stifled a yawn. She was tired; the concert had been going on a long time and it was hot in the big hall which was packed to suffocation.

Not only were there people seated on all the small, hard, gilt chairs, but there were even others grouped around the walls, all sitting with that look of polite boredom on their faces which she felt was visible on her own.

It seemed to her a century ago since they had left the Duflot house for the big luncheon about which Jeanne had spoken to her the day before.

Varia had thought that it would be a large luncheon party, but she had not expected nearly three hundred to sit down, and she had certainly not expected the formality and the speeches.

The latter were interminable. There were toasts which were proposed and replied to, and the Chairman of the luncheon, who was Monsieur Duflot, had a great deal to say and took an extremely long time in saying it.

Ian was the sixth speaker. He spoke in English and she was surprised when he began, to see that he was quite at ease.

She would have expected him to be embarrassed and rather tongue-tied, but instead he astonished her by being fluent, and extremely able in all he had to say.

When the luncheon was over she had hoped to escape; but she found, instead, that the whole party was going on to the concert to be held in the Municipal Hall in aid of one of the charities of the Silk Organisation.

It was a very highbrow and formal concert, with pianist succeeding operatic singer, violinist and a quartet which played classical music of the most untuneful sort.

It was nearly six o'clock before the last performer bowed to the perfunctory applause and the band struck up the *Marseillaise*.

With relief the audience vacated the hall and Varia found herself, like everyone else, taking deep breaths of fresh air when they reached the steps outside.

"The cars will be waiting for us," Monsieur Duflot said.

"I will take Varia with me," Ian remarked.

She felt his hand give a pull on her arm. She turned gratefully and they ran, almost like children who were escaping from school, to where the sports car he had rented was parked at the side of the building.

"Thank God that's over!" Ian said as he got in.

"I hope we are not going to have any more celebrations of this sort," Varia remarked.

"Dozens of them," he replied. "Tonight we are dining with the Mayor and then there is a Ball afterwards for which many silk dresses have been designed by French *couturiers*."

"That sounds rather fun," Varia said.

"I'm glad you think so," he answered. "Personally, I would pay never to see a silk dress again. If I ever have a wife, I shall forbid her to wear anything but cotton."

There was a note of bitterness in his voice which Varia could not help noticing, but there was no time to say more.

Ian was drawing up outside a large hotel with a big courtyard where there were a number of other cars parked. He got out and helped her to alight.

"Let's go inside and relax by ourselves," he said. "I don't think I can face the Duflot's again until I have had a very

138

strong whisky and soda."

The lounge of the hotel had a huge window looking over a flower-filled garden. Varia settled herself on a comfortable sofa by an open window, and pulled off her hat.

It was very light but she wanted to feel free and relaxed, and taking a comb from her bag she combed her short curls until they danced around her head like little tongues of golden fire.

Ian was ordering.

"Do you want tea?" he enquired. "Or would you like something stronger?"

"Tea, please," Varia answered.

"With milk or lemon, *Madame?*" the waiter asked.

"Milk, please," Varia replied. She heard Ian order a large whisky and soda.

"You ought to be drinking wine in France," she said.

"When I'm abroad, I feel particularly British," he answered. "I have a yearning for roast beef and apple tart, and whisky instead of any form of wine, however good."

She laughed at that and he added seriously:

"I'm afraid I'm a rebel against things that are expected of me. Don't you ever feel like that?"

"Yes, I do," she admitted. "But I shouldn't

139

have expected it of you."

"Why?" he enquired. "Do I look so dull?"

"Not exactly dull," she answered frankly. "But conventional."

"If I am, it's because I have to be," he said.

Again there was that bitterness in his voice she could not quite account for.

"By the way," he said before she could make any reply. "We may not have to stay here as long as I anticipate. I had a long talk with Monsieur Duflot this morning. He agrees to everything that was stipulated in my father's contract. As soon as it's signed, there's no reason why we shouldn't go home."

Now that she was faced with the thought of returning home sooner than she had anticipated, Varia felt almost regretful. She thought of those lovely dresses hanging up in the wardrobe which she might not have the opportunity of wearing.

At that moment the waiter arrived back with her tea and Ian's drink.

He was setting it down on the table when Varia looked across the lounge and saw a number of people coming in through the door.

They had coats over their arms, small travelling bags in their hands, and she guessed that either a train or an aeroplane had just arrived and these were the passengers from it.

Another newcomer came in through the door and moved slowly, with an exquisite grace, towards the reception desk.

It was her clothes that Varia noticed first — a beautifully cut suit of honey-coloured shantung, a pale blond mink coat over her arms, shoes and gloves to match and a hat that was only a wisp of tulle and ribbon to halo the red curls dancing round her white forehead.

She must have given a little gasp at the sight of Lareen, or perhaps the fixity of her gaze drew Ian's attention.

At any rate, he looked up and saw the direction of her eyes and she felt him stiffen.

"Lareen!" he said beneath his breath.

"You weren't expecting her?" Varia asked.

"No, no, of course not," he said — "Listen, Varia! There's going to be trouble. Stand by me. Don't let me down."

For the first time since they had met, he seemed to her completely and absolutely human — a young man in trouble, a man who needed help, rather than an autocrat giving orders.

"But . . . of course I'll . . . help you," she stammered. "But . . . how?"

There was no reply. Lareen had seen them, and turning away from the reception desk, she walked slowly towards them, her face set, her red lips tightly compressed into a thin line.

She reached them and stood looking down at them for a second before Ian rose to his feet.

"Lareen!" he said in a voice of surprise. "I didn't expect to see you here."

"I bet you didn't," Lareen said in a rather ugly tone.

Varia realised that her voice was rather common and out of tune with her elegant appearance.

"Won't you sit down?" Ian asked. "You know Varia, I think."

Lareen didn't even glance towards her. She sat down in the chair next to Ian and looked into her handbag.

Slowly she seemed to grapple with a number of things that the bag contained until, finally, she drew out something which Varia could see at once was a cutting from a newspaper.

She held it out towards Ian.

"I've come here," she said, "to ask for an explanation of this."

Ian took it from her and Varia, without appearing to look closely, could see quite clearly the headline: *"Engagement of Silk King's Son."*

It was obviously cut from some gossip column and then, as Ian appeared to read it carefully, Lareen said impatiently:

"Well, what have you got to say for yourself?"

"What is there to say?" Ian asked slowly.

Lareen's green eyes seemed to shoot out sparks of fire.

"A great deal, I should think," she answered. "When did this happen? Why didn't you tell me? How could you let me learn about it from the newspapers?"

"It was all rather complicated to explain . . ." Ian began.

"I don't want to hear a lot of lies," Lareen interrupted. "Where did you meet this girl? Why haven't I seen her with you before?"

"Varia is a very old friend of the family," Ian said. "My father knew her mother many years ago."

"So that's it, is it?" Lareen said sharply. "This is one of your father's tricks. Oh, well! He was determined to get you away from me and now he's succeeded. I thought you had enough guts to stand up to him. Apparently you're weak and spineless and just as crafty as he is when it comes to avoiding anything unpleasant."

It was obvious that Lareen was working herself up into almost a frenzy and Ian said soothingly:

"Please, Lareen, let me try to explain."

"You're not going to get away with this," Lareen went on. "Don't think it for a moment. You've taken me out all winter and made sure that everyone in London knew that you were my young man. And now, without a word, without saying anything, you announce your engagement to someone else. What can she give you that I can't?"

"I don't think we need bring Miss Milfield into this," Ian said frigidly.

"Like hell we won't!" Lareen answered. "She's in it, isn't she? And therefore she can hear a few home-truths. Does she know what she's marrying, I wonder? Does she know what a coward you are where your father's concerned? How you're nothing more or less than a slave to his slightest whim? Have you told her all that?"

She paused for breath, then went on:

"Or perhaps your father approves of her and that means there'll be no need for you to do anything but go on being frightened of the old man and toadying to his every whim."

"Lareen, I won't have you talking like this," Ian said, with some semblance of dignity.

"And how are you going to stop me?" Lareen asked. "You're not going to be able to. And I'll tell you something else. If you don't break off this ridiculous engagement immediately, then I'm going to start proceedings for breach of promise! We'll see how you and that old dictator you call your father will like that. It won't look very well in the papers, will it? It's not the sort of publicity that does anyone any good."

She almost snarled the last words as she rose to her feet and stood, it seemed to Varia, towering above them.

"I shall be here in the hotel," she said to Ian. "If you know what's good for you, you'll come and talk turkey."

She slung her handbag over her arm and then turned to Varia.

"As for you," she said. "You'd better leave him alone, unless you want that pretty face of yours scratched until it's hardly recognisable. And when I make threats I don't make idle ones either!"

She turned on her heel and walked away from them, leaving Varia staring after her in absolute astonishment, and Ian with a frown between his eyes.

They watched her without either of them moving, until she reached the reception desk. And then, suddenly, with an effort, as if he awoke from a dream, Ian was galvanised into action.

He took several hundred franc notes out of his pocket and put them down on the table. Then he rose to his feet and said just two words.

"Come along!"

Varia followed him obediently, moving so quickly that she had the greatest difficulty in keeping up with him. Ian walked from the hotel and out to the car.

He opened the door and Varia got in and he started up the engine and, driving at a furious pace as if it somehow relieved his mind, he turned the car away from the city, out into the open country.

They drove for perhaps five miles in silence until they came to a pretty road bordered by trees, and stopped some way along it where a little below them the river Saône moved slowly between high banks.

Ian switched off the engine and sat staring ahead of him, saying nothing.

After some time Varia said a little timidly:

"What are you going to do?"

"I don't know," he answered.

"Will she really do what she says," Varia

asked, "and bring a breach of promise action against you?"

"She may try," he answered. "She won't succeed. I've never proposed marriage to her. She can't prove that I have. But she can make things very uncomfortable." He gave a little sigh. "It's all so vulgar."

Varia thought personally that Lareen was very vulgar, but she didn't like to say so. And after a moment's pause she asked gently:

"Do you love her very much?"

"Love her!" The words came out of Ian's mouth like an explosion. "No, of course not!"

"Then, I don't understand," Varia said. "Why does she think so? Why have you been so much with her?"

"Because I am a fool," Ian answered. "Because I am all the things she's accused me of — and a great many more besides. Oh, hell! Why should I bother you with this?"

He spoke with an emotion that she had never expected of him.

Gone was the reserved, stiff young man whom Sarah had once called "Mr. Shirty," and in his place was someone who was suffering, someone who, it seemed to Varia, was obviously unhappy.

"I'm sorry," she said simply. "I wish I could help you."

Ian turned his head and looked at her.

"Do you mean that?" he asked.

"Yes, of course," she answered. "You are in trouble. I don't know why, but you are, aren't you?"

"I'm in a hole," he confessed. "I can't tell you about it. I can't tell anyone."

"I understand," Varia said sympathetically. "But I wish I could be of some use. Telling another person sometimes straightens things out."

"Do you want to know because you are just curious? Or because you really want to help me?" he asked surprisingly.

"Because I want to help you," she answered.

He looked at her for a long moment. There was something in his eyes she didn't understand, an expression she had never seen there before.

Then very quietly he said:

"Thank you, Varia. You have helped me," and switched on the engine.

"Thank you for a lovely evening," Varia said to Monsieur Duflot, and meant it in all sincerity.

She had not expected to enjoy the Ball,

feeling that she would be shy and would know no-one. But as so often happens when in anticipation we are convinced a party will be disappointing, Varia had loved every minute of it.

To begin with, the surroundings were magnificent. The big rooms, filled with flowers and glittering chandeliers looked as if they belonged to another age; and the guests all wearing their best clothes, were as colourful and as gorgeous as their surroundings.

What Varia enjoyed more than anything was the Dress Show, which exhibited some of the wonderful materials that were made in Lyons.

It was impossible to visualise a more wonderful array of gowns than those worn by the pretty models, who also showed fabulous jewellery and a wealth of fine furs.

When the Dress Show was over everyone danced and Varia found, to her surprise, that she was a success.

There seemed to be dozens of young men only too anxious to dance with her; and when finally Ian, in duty bound, asked her for a foxtrot, he was too late; she was already promised six dances ahead and could not fit him in.

It was strange, she thought to herself, how

quickly one got used to being looked at.

She didn't even feel embarrassed as her partner whirled her round the room and she realised that everyone was watching, pointing her out as the young English girl who was staying with the Duflots.

The fact was that Varia didn't feel that they were looking at her but at her dress.

Martin Myles had definitely excelled himself. The heavy white satin, which was obviously a product from Lyons had been embroidered with garlands of forget-me-nots and rosebuds, all executed in coloured stones and diamanté.

There was a deep hem of forget-me-not blue and the same colour formed the base of the glittering shoulder-straps which held the tiny, sparkling bodice and cascaded away in a veritable stream of beautiful embroiders down her back to the floor.

The wide skirts were held in place with a crinoline which made her waist look tiny, but which, in taking up so much floor space, made it impossible for anyone not to notice her.

She wondered where Lareen was and felt thankful that because this was a private Ball there was no chance of her appearing and making yet another scene.

When Varia thought of what had occurred at the hotel that afternoon, she felt quite sick at the embarrassment and the shock of it.

'What would Mummy have thought?' she said to herself.

She knew that her sweet, gentle mother would be not only disgusted at Lareen but upset that she, Varia, should be involved in such vulgarity.

The thought of her mother made Varia forget everything else.

She hoped that she would get a letter from Switzerland tomorrow, for she had sent her mother a telegram telling her of her visit to Lyons; she had followed it with a letter to explain that she was going on a special journey at the request of Sir Edward.

As she wrote the loving words which accompanied the somewhat laboured explanation, she was ashamed because she was not telling her mother the whole truth.

She had written her another letter tonight before she dressed for the dinner, telling her how much she loved her and begging her to get well quickly.

It had nearly made her late, especially as she and Ian had not returned to the house until nearly quarter-past seven. But with a tremendous effort Varia managed to be downstairs just as the clock in the hall struck eight o'clock.

Dinner had been rather boring because the men were elderly friends of Monsieur Duflot and could talk of little else but trade. But the Ball made up for everything.

"It was lovely! Absolutely lovely!" Varia cried now to Madame Duflot.

"We are relieved you enjoyed it," Madame Duflot said. "We were rather afraid that anyone who came from London, from the gay society you meet there, would find our little gala evening rather provincial."

Varia could not help smiling. She wondered what the Duflots would say if they knew she had never been to a Ball.

"Good night!" she said again to everyone.

Because she knew that it was expected of her, she stood in front of Ian and held up her cheek to be kissed.

She tried to be poised and sophisticated about it, but at the moment of nearness her worldliness disappeared suddenly, she felt the blood rising in her cheeks, a quickening of the heart.

One moment she felt paralysed as if she could not move, the next she wanted to run and run.

Then she felt his lips somewhere near her left ear, and she turned away from him with

152

a swirl of her full skirts.

It was over; the tumult in her breasts and the colour in her cheeks were subsiding as quickly as they had arisen. It was easier to breathe again.

'Why should he make me feel like that?' she asked herself and because there was no answer, she forced the question aside.

"Bonne nuit, Madame! Bonne nuit, Jeanne!" she said at the door of her room, and having entered and switched on the light, shut the door behind her.

"You were a success! You really were a success!" she told her reflection on the other side of the room.

She laughed at her thoughts and turned towards the dressing-table. As she did so, she saw there was an envelope lying on her pillow. For a moment she stared at it and then she crossed quickly to pick it up.

There was no need to guess who it was from. She had only seen that thick, rather dashing writing once before, but she would have recognised it anywhere. She opened the envelope.

"I must see you. I have tried to get hold of you all day but you have always been out. Come through the side door whatever time you get in, or I swear I shall come and fetch you. Pierre."

Varia smiled at that. Come and fetch her, indeed! He wouldn't dare. And yet, she was not so sure. He was capable of doing anything in his impetuosity.

"Well, I can't see him and that's that," she said aloud.

At the same time she felt a little pang of regret in her heart that he should not see her looking as she did now.

If he had thought her attractive when they met in the Park, what would he think of her in this glorious dress, with her cheeks flushed with excitement, her eyes shining like stars?

"No, no," she said aloud. "You are not going. You know you can't. You promised; you gave your word."

As she spoke there was a knock on the door.

"Who is it?" she asked, forgetting to speak in French.

The door opened very softly. It was the little maid who stood there.

"What is it, Annette?" Varia asked.

"C'est Monsieur le Comte, Ma'm'selle."

"Is he outside?" Varia enquired.

"Oui, Ma'm'selle, and it is imperative that you should speak with him."

"Well, I cannot do so. Tell him it is impossible," Varia said.

Annette looked ready to cry.

"Oh. *Ma'm'selle,* if you do not go to him

he will make a scene. He has threatened to come into the house. I shall lose my job. *Madame* will find out that I have taken his money and she will dismiss me. Oh, please, *Ma'm'selle,* come and speak to him. He is very impatient."

"I really cannot . . ." Varia started to say, then saw the tears in Annette's eyes and realised that she could not hurt this poor little servant girl.

"Very well," she said. "But for goodness sake don't let *Madame* hear us."

"No, no, *Ma'm'selle.* And it would be best if you came down the back stairs. It is less dangerous that way."

With Annette leading the way, Varia tiptoed across the landing and through a door at the far end which led to the back stairs.

She had to lift her skirts high and hold them close against her so as to negotiate the narrow, uncovered, wooden stairway which led down to the kitchen quarters.

They doubled back along a narrow corridor to the side door. Annette opened it and immediately, as if he had been standing just outside, Pierre stepped into the house.

"Merci," he said to Annette, and pressed some crackling notes into her hand.

"Merci beaucoup, M'sieur!"

Annette vanished into the shadows of the

passage and Pierre turned towards Varia.

"You look wonderful!" he said with almost an awed note in his voice. "Come for a drive, *chérie*. I want to talk to you."

"I can't," she said.

"*Mon Dieu,* but I insist. If you won't, I shall carry you, and that will make a terrible noise and perhaps arouse the household."

"Oh, Pierre!" Varia put her fingers up to her temples. "Please don't make a scene. I don't think I could bear another one today."

"Another one?" His voice was curious.

"Yes," Varia answered. "I've already been involved in one terrible row."

"Who made that?" he enquired.

"Oh nobody you would know," Varia answered. "Just an English model who is staying in the hotel. Her name is Lareen."

"Lareen? Do you mean to say Lareen is here in Lyons?"

"Do you know her?" Varia asked.

She had referred to Lareen, first, because she really genuinely felt she could not bear another scene, and secondly, because to talk of something else gave her time to decide how she could best get rid of Pierre.

"*Mais oui!* Of course I know Lareen," Pierre answered. "And I know a great many things about her that she would not like anyone else to know, too."

156

"What are they?" Varia asked quickly.

"Nothing to her advantage and a great many things to her disadvantage," Pierre answered. "But let's talk about us."

"No, I want to talk about Lareen," Varia insisted.

"Then come for a drive and I will tell you about her," Pierre tempted.

She knew exactly what he was doing. At the same time, while she had already determined not to go with him, she began to weaken.

Perhaps he really had got some information which would be of value to Ian. It seemed the long hand of coincidence, but things in life often happen that way.

If Lareen was really going to blackmail Ian, well, the more he knew about her the easier it might be for him to prevent her causing a scandal.

"If I come with you," Varia said cautiously, "will you really tell me about Lareen? That is if you have anything to tell. Perhaps you are just pretending."

"No, I am not pretending," Pierre said. "If you will come with me I will tell you anything you want to know."

"Promise?" Varia questioned.

"I promise," he replied. "And now, come along. The car is here."

"I must be careful of this dress," she said.

If she had known what was going to happen, she would have taken it off and put on something more suitable. But even when she had thought of this she knew it would have been a hard thing to do because she had wanted Pierre to see her.

They were exceeding all speed limits through the empty streets.

There was no-one about and in a very few minutes they were out in the empty countryside, with the wind blowing through the trees and the stars already paling a little in the darkness of the sky.

"Where are you going?" she asked breathlessly.

"I am taking you to my château," he answered.

"No, no," she cried. "I told you last night that I would not go in."

"That was last night," he answered with a grin. "Tonight I am going to insist. I don't want you to see it. I want it to see you. *La pauvre maison* will think it is back in the past with some glorious lady of the Court moving through the rooms."

Then, before she could protest at the highhanded way in which he was taking her there, they had turned down the long, tree-bordered drive and the beautiful château stood waiting for them.

"I had a feeling that you might come here tonight," he said, getting out of the car. "I know that I ought to have strewn the steps with rose petals, but there is a bottle of champagne waiting for you in the Salon."

"I ought not to come in," Varia said, sitting still, though he had opened the door beside her.

"Just for a few minutes," he pleaded. "Just while I tell you what you want to know about Lareen, and while you see where I live — and why."

"Why!" Varia echoed.

"Because I love this house," he answered, "more than any other that I own or could wish to own. Come and look for yourself."

He was tempting her and somehow she could not refuse.

Varia let him lead her in through the big, arched door of the château. It was cool and dark inside the Hall. Varia waited until Pierre switched on the lights and then she saw that it was, indeed, very beautiful.

Taking her arm, Pierre led her from the Hall into an ante-room hung with exquisite tapestries and through that into a long, low room with French windows opening onto the garden, which she recognised must be the Salon.

The panelled walls, painted in exquisite colours — grey, blue and pink, were a frame for the long, gilt-encrusted mirrors and, what Varia knew instinctively was a fabulous collection of valuable china.

There were curtains in a soft rose pink, the gilt chairs were covered with fine needlework, and the Aubusson carpet was a riot of roses.

"It's lovely!" Varia exclaimed almost involuntarily.

"As lovely as you," he replied. "That is why I wanted you both to meet."

He crossed the room to where, on a table, she saw there was a bottle of champagne and two glasses.

"You were so certain I would come," she said accusingly as he started to open the bottle.

"I always get what I want," he replied. "You will find that out in time."

"I shall do my best to stop your being so conceited," Varia retorted. "Now tell me about Lareen."

"*Bien,*" he said, pouring her out a glass of champagne. "I will keep my part of the bargain, but you are not to cheat by running away the very second I have done so. Tell me, first, why are you so interested in Lareen?"

"She's threatening to blackmail a . . . a friend of mine."

Pierre laughed again.

"Up to her old tricks, is she? She's a dangerous customer unless you know how to handle her."

"And how would you do that?" Varia enquired.

"By being in the position to blackmail her first," Pierre replied.

"But how?" Varia asked.

He sipped his champagne and walked across to lean on the mantelpiece. Varia seated herself on a sofa covered in needlework.

"I knew Lareen first before she was famous," Pierre said. "She came out to Morocco where my father had some property, and we all thought she was one of the loveliest girls we had ever seen."

"To Morocco!" Varia exclaimed. "What was she doing there?"

"She had just married the eldest son of our overseer. He met her in France and told her that he was a prince living the most fabulous and romantic life. Because he was very attractive, in a dark Arab way, she believed him."

"And Lareen married him!" Varia exclaimed.

"Oh, yes! They were married in a Catholic church so there was no question of divorce, even when Lareen found that both the title and her husband's palace were merely figments of his imagination."

"What happened?" Varia asked.

"She left, of course. She got some business man who came out to Morocco to take her home with him. He was very infatuated, I believe, but her only use for him was that he should pay her fare to Paris. Then she went to England and I lost sight of her."

"So Lareen is married!" Varia said quietly, realising what this would mean to Ian.

"Certainement," Pierre replied. "I was enquiring of her father-in-law only recently what he was going to do about the marriage, and he asked me, rather pathetically I thought, what could be done. The marriage is binding, both legally and morally — though I don't think that has stopped the young man from setting up quite a harem of other Lareens!"

Varia gave a deep sigh. This information could save Ian from any fear of scandal or gossip.

What was more, as a married woman Lareen would be unable to start an action for a breach of promise if she had ever really intended to do so.

162

"Thank you for telling me," Varia said quietly, setting down her glass after she had taken two small sips.

Pierre came towards her as he spoke and sitting down beside her put his arms around her.

"No!" Varia said quickly.

But she was too late.

He drew her easily to him, his arms encircling her, and as he did so she realised how big he was and how small and helpless she was in comparison.

"Pierre, we must go back," she said quickly.

"Not yet," he answered. "Not until you have paid me for the information I have given you."

"I didn't think this was part of the bargain."

She started to speak lightly, at the same time she was conscious that her heart had begun to beat rather quickly.

All too late she realised how mad it was of her to have come here alone — alone in a bachelor establishment in the middle of the night.

"Please, Pierre," she said. "I want to look round this room. I want you to tell me about the picture over there."

She pointed behind him as she spoke and

instinctively he turned his head. And in that second she was free.

Rising, she moved across to inspect another picture which hung between two windows.

"This also is charming," she said, striving to keep her voice low and unflurried. "Who painted it?"

"We don't really know," Pierre answered. "Although we like to think it is a Watteau. It is one of my ancestors, and rather an attractive one."

"She is lovely," Varia said quickly, and turned again because she realised he was standing very close to her.

"Is that Sèvres?" she enquired. "The big vase, I mean."

Before he could answer she had turned again, moving away down the room in the direction in which they had just come. She stopped at a big writing-desk in front of one of the windows.

It looked suspiciously tidy, as if no-one worked at it very often. But on it was a large picture in a gilt frame of a rather attractive girl with a magnolia in her dark hair.

"Who is that?" Varia asked for something to say, only too conscious that silence between her and Pierre was dangerous.

"Who?" Pierre asked, as if he was

thinking of something else.

Then, as Varia pointed to the photograph, he said:

"Oh, that is Marie Christian, my *fiancée*."

"Your what?" In her surprise Varia turned round to face him. "What did you say?"

"My *fiancée*," he answered. "Don't be so astonished. You have your *fiancé*, I have mine. What is the difference?"

For a moment Varia was tongue-tied. She had forgotten that he might know about Ian. She was, at the same time, utterly bowled over by the fact that he was engaged to another woman.

Many things she had expected, but not this.

Pierre laughed down at her.

"I know what you are thinking," he said. "It is quite unnecessary. You see, my dear, Marie and I have been betrothed to each other since we were children. It is an arrangement which was made by our fathers because our estates march with one another. She is very charming and we are *très bons amis*. Sometime — this year, next year, perhaps the year after — we shall get married. But in the meantime, we are both enjoying ourselves — she in her way and I in mine. Now do you understand?"

"Yes . . . I suppose so," Varia answered. "But . . . but I want to go . . . home. It is getting late."

She did not know why, but she felt suddenly repulsed at the very idea of being here. She wanted to get away. She wanted to be back in the security of that quiet little room in the Duflots' house.

"And suppose I don't let you go?" Pierre said in a low voice.

She turned round only to find herself in his arms.

"Please, Pierre, don't be silly!"

"I believe you are annoyed that I'm engaged!" he accused her. "If you are, it is the greatest compliment that has ever been paid me. I didn't know that you liked me enough to be jealous of me."

"But I'm not! I'm not!" Varia said.

She knew that what she said was not the truth, but that it was almost impossible to put her real feelings into words.

"You are jealous," Pierre taunted. "So, *ma petite,* I must show you how unnecessary it is? For my heart — yes, my whole heart — is yours for the taking?"

He bent his head as he spoke and before she could prevent him, before she could move or even struggle, his lips were on hers.

166

Then he was kissing her wildly, passionately, possessively, in what seemed like an almost uncontrollable frenzy.

"No, Pierre! No!" she cried at last, struggling ineffectively with trembling hands to push him away.

But now he was kissing her shoulders and the little hollow between her breasts.

"No! No! Please . . . let me . . . go. I want to . . . go."

The last words were lost as he swept her closer, still staring down at her face, his eyes aflame, his lips only an inch from her own bruised and quivering mouth.

"Do you think I can let you go now?" he asked hoarsely. "*Je t'adore*. I love you, Varia! I want you! I knew when you came here tonight that I could make you stay. We are going to be so happy, so very happy, *ma petite chou,* my little princess."

"No! No!" Varia tried to say again.

He stopped her mouth with kisses, holding her arms pinioned by his so that it was impossible for her to struggle against him.

She felt as if he dragged her down into the dark frightening depths of a sea of passion from which there was no escape.

His kisses seemed to sap her strength and her power of thought, and a long, long way away she could hear his voice, triumphant and exulting.

"I love you! You are glorious, wonderful, adorable! A little white flower. This is our night of love — *une nuit de gloire*."

"No! No! Pierre . . . let me . . . go. Please . . . let me . . . go!"

His kisses were wilder and more possessive than ever. They seemed literally to bruise her skin, to leave her quivering, not only with fear but with pain.

Suddenly he bent down and lifted her in his arms.

"I will carry you upstairs," he said. "*La nuit,* my little rose, is still ours."

She gave a scream then — a scream of sheer terror. But when it came from her lips it sounded little more than a whimper of fear, such as a child might make.

"I can't . . . I can't!" she tried to say.

But the words seemed strangled in her throat.

"You are mine!" Pierre answered.

He held her high in his arms, her dress was crumpled by his strength, some of the diamanté and coloured stones falling onto the carpet around them to lie there twinkling in the lights like teardrops.

She saw the passion burning in his eyes, heard the wildness of his tone, and knew that he was past any appeal for mercy.

With a sense almost of despair, she cried out again, and knew, even as she heard her own voice that it was quite useless.

Pierre was moving towards the door.

Then even as he did so, there was a sudden sound behind them, one of the French windows was pushed open and a voice, calm, flat and very English, said:

"I apologise if I appear to intrude, but I think it is time I took Varia home."

Chapter Five

For a moment Pierre seemed bereft of speech.

Then as Ian came through the French windows and moved a little way into the Salon he said:

"*Nom de diable!* Who are you and what the hell do you mean by coming here?"

"I followed you," Ian said quietly. "I had no desire to interfere with my *fiancée* making a friendly visit to your house so long as it remained . . . friendly."

There was something ominous in the way he said the last words.

Very slowly, almost as if he were moving in a slow motion film, Pierre put Varia down on the floor.

She stood for a moment, trembling; and then, because she was very near to fainting, she sat down on the nearest chair and put her hands up to her face.

She felt not only weak but bruised from

the passion and the pain of Pierre's kisses and because he had done something to her spirit, leaving her for the moment in a vacuum of emotional feelings so that she felt as if everything that happened was far away and that she was no longer a part of it.

Almost in a dream she heard Ian say, with a sudden sharpness in his voice:

"Good Lord! It's de Chalayat, isn't it?"

"That is my name," Pierre retorted with a touch of pride. "And now, may I request you to get out of here before I throw you out?"

"I think you would find that rather difficult," Ian answered. "But, as it happens, I have every intention of leaving and taking Miss Milfield with me. But before I go there is one thing I want to say to you — something which I have always promised myself the pleasure of saying should we ever meet. And that is that I consider you an unprincipled and totally despicable cad and bounder!"

There was so much venom and anger in Ian's voice that in sheer astonishment Varia took her hands from her face and stared at him.

She saw the two men facing each other almost like fighting cocks braced up for the assault.

They were about equal height, but while Pierre had the grace and wiriness of his race, Ian was heavily built with the kind of dependable stability which is so typically British.

"Would it be presumptuous," Pierre enquired with an almost amused note in his voice, "to ask why I am privileged to receive such a token of your esteem?"

"You may certainly ask it," Ian said. "I happen to be a friend of Lettice Durham and her family."

Varia saw Pierre start and his eyes flicker.

It was only a momentary reaction, for almost instantly he said lightly:

"Lettice Durham! I don't think I know the name."

"I think you do," Ian answered through his teeth. "And this, de Chalayat, is where your lies will not help you. Lettice, as you well know, killed herself because of the way you treated her."

"It's a lie," Pierre said, but somehow his denial was not convincing.

"It's the truth," Ian answered. "And if any man deserves to stand in the dock for murder, you do."

"*Mon Dieu,* I am not going to let you insult me in my own house!" Pierre exclaimed furiously. "Get out and stay out."

"The obvious retort of an absolute outsider," Ian said. "And I'll go because I don't wish to soil my feet by walking on any property that belongs to you. But before I go I am going to give you something which you should have received a long time ago, if you'd had your deserts — and that is a good hiding."

He stepped forward as he spoke and almost involuntarily Varia gave a little scream, for he lunged out at Pierre and caught him a heavy blow on the right cheek.

Varia heard the dull impact of flesh meeting flesh, and then Pierre struck back, catching Ian on the side of the ear.

From that moment they were fighting in earnest.

The room was filled with the sound of their heavy breathing and the crash of a small table covered in valuable *objets d'art* which Pierre overturned as he stepped backwards.

Thud! Thud! Both men, equally matched it seemed, were raining blows on each other.

Varia, after that first scream, felt as if she were paralysed. She could not move; in fact she could hardly breathe. She could only watch, with her hands tightly clasped together, her lips parted, her eyes wide in terror.

Never before in her life had she seen two men fighting, and there was something strangely horrible in the earnestness with which these two attacked each other relentlessly.

A blow from Ian brought the blood spurting from Pierre's nose. His lip was already bleeding, and Varia realised that he was taking the greater punishment of the two.

Quite suddenly his guard slipped and Ian gave him a terrific uppercut under the chin.

For a moment he seemed to stand there suspended, as it were, in midair.

Then without a sound coming from his lips he fell backwards, crashing against the desk and crumpling upon the floor beside it.

He was out!

Ian stood looking down at him. His breath came wheezingly from between his parted lips, and Varia saw that the knuckles of his right hand were bleeding.

He straightened his bow tie, took a handkerchief from his breast pocket and wrapped it round his hand.

"Come along," he said abruptly.

"Are you going to leave him like this?" Varia asked.

"If there was a dung heap I'd chuck him into it," Ian replied. "Are you coming or do you wish to stay with him?"

His question was harsh and brutal and brought the blood flowing back into Varia's pale cheeks.

"I'm coming with you," she answered in a low voice.

"Very well, then, let's go."

Ian crossed the room ahead of her to push open the French window where it had swung to in the wind.

There was a path which led to the front of the house where the cars were waiting, and Varia realised how easy it had been for Ian to find his way to the Salon and to listen outside to what was going on without either her or Pierre being aware of his presence.

In silence he helped her into the front of his car and then got in himself. As he did so, she glanced at him sideways.

Never had she seen him look so grim, so stern, so completely withdrawn into himself as if he were hardly aware of her presence.

Ian started up the car and they set off at a great speed as if he was anxious to put the château far behind him in the shortest amount of time possible.

She heard the wind whistling past them and knew that even if she had wished to talk it would have been impossible for her words would have been lost.

Indeed, she wondered a little faintly if there was anything she could say.

He despised her and because it was so obvious by his expression and in the very atmosphere about him, she began to despise herself too.

How she could have been so stupid, so foolish, to think for a moment that Pierre really loved her?

Wasn't he just the type of philandering Frenchman about whom girls had been warned from time immemorial?

She felt her spirits drop into the depths of self condemnation. Despondency encompassed her like a cloud and she felt perilously near to tears.

Ian drew up the car a little way down the street from the Duflots' front door; then he turned towards her and looked at her, it seemed to Varia, for the first time since he had entered the château.

"You little fool!" he said furiously. "How could you have trusted a man like that?"

Varia opened her lips to speak, to tell him why she had gone to the château. But Ian was not waiting for her explanation.

"I suppose you'd never heard of de Chalayat?" he asked. "But even if you hadn't, you would have thought that any girl who had been decently brought up would have known that he was a bounder and a cad of the very first water."

He gave an exasperated, angry sigh, and then went on:

"I suppose, enamoured with his love-making, swept off your idiotic little feet by his compliments, you had to go creeping out after him tonight even after your promise to me. Well, if that's the type of man you want, you'd better have him. I'll get you back to London as soon as I can. That will fulfill my part of the bargain and then, if you want to continue to run after de Chalayat, you can pay your own fare back to France."

Ian slapped his hand down on the wheel of the car.

"I daresay he will be pleased to see you — to treat you as he has treated other women, by taking all they have to give and chucking them away as soon as he is bored or a prettier face turns up to divert his attentions."

It wasn't so much what he was saying but the violent and utterly contemptuous manner in which he said it.

The whole misery of what she had been through in the past hour welled up in Varia's throat to choke her.

She couldn't answer; she couldn't say anything; she could only fight against her tears.

Fumblingly she put out her hand to find the handle of the door. Then, without saying anything, without trying to justify her actions, she scrambled out of the car onto the pavement and ran towards the Duflots' house in a blind, unreasoning effort to get away from Ian.

When she had reached the side door out of which she had come, she had to stop and fumble in her bag for the key.

It took her a moment to find it and just as she had it in her hand Ian caught up with her. He reached out and took the key from her, inserted it in the lock and opened the door.

Varia stepped forward into the cool darkness of the house.

For a moment she hesitated, wondering which way to go, forgetting for a moment where the back stairs were down which Annette had brought her to meet Pierre.

She heard Ian shut the door behind them and then as she turned away from him instinctively in flight, his arms reached out and caught hold of her shoulders.

"You poor little idiot," she heard him say in a very different tone of voice from what he had used to her before. "You didn't know what you were up against. I suppose it all seemed to you very glamorous and romantic."

To her consternation Varia felt the tears running down her cheeks. She didn't know why, but Ian's kindness was harder to bear than his anger.

It was impossible for her to speak, impossible to say anything. She could only stand there dumbly because he was holding her.

She couldn't see him. There was only the vague silhouette of his head and shoulders against the daylight which, mingled with the glow from the street light, percolated through the fanlight over the door.

"Romantic! That, I suppose, is what de Chalayat is," Ian said with an ironic wistfulness under his sarcasm, and added: "But if it's kisses you are looking for, my poor innocent, what's wrong with English ones?"

Blinded by her tears, Varia had no idea what he was about until she felt his fingers tilting up her chin. Then suddenly his mouth was on hers and he kissed her — a quiet, deep, somehow surprisingly gentle kiss.

A kiss which seemed to check her tears and to put everything else from her mind except the surprise of it.

Then almost before she could realise what was happening she was free.

"Go to bed," she heard Ian's voice say.

He had turned from her and opening the

door onto the street had passed through it, pulling it to behind him with a little click.

She stood where he had left her, too bewildered for the moment to do anything but stare after him. *He had kissed her!*.

She could not understand why her mouth felt so strange. She could only stare at the closed door, and slowly, almost reluctantly, walk upstairs to her bedroom.

In her own room, she closed the door and instead of switching on the light, in the darkness from the curtained windows she groped her way to the bed and threw herself face downwards, hiding her face in the pillow.

Thinking — thinking — thinking; letting the events of the evening roar over her like immense waves, each one leaving her more battered and breathless than the one before.

And yet, through the chaos and tumult of her thoughts, one thing remained almost like a beacon of calmness and peace. Ian's kiss! It had not been the kiss of a man who is angry, or even a man who is contemptuous.

It was something else, something she did not understand, which in some extraordinary way had been like the touch of cooling fingers on a feverish brow.

It had calmed her; it had swept away her tears and misery and humiliation.

It had even made her forget, for a moment, the horror of Pierre's kisses, of his experienced hands, of the lust in his eyes which had terrified her more than she had ever been terrified in her life before.

She had believed that to be love — fool, fool that she was. Fool to have trusted him even for a moment. And what if Ian had not come in time?

The full realisation of the debt of gratitude that she owed Ian came flooding over her in a crimson wave of embarrassment which made not only her cheeks but her whole body burn at the thought of what he must think of her.

No wonder he was contemptuous. No wonder he despised her. No wonder he had thought her cheap and wanton.

She flushed again in the darkness; and then, as she sank down into the very depths of self accusation, she felt again his kiss, so soothing, so gentle upon her tortured mouth.

She must have slept a little with her own thoughts running through it. Thoughts which had become feelings that were nothing more or less than accusing thought.

Suddenly there was a knock on the door. Varia raised her head.

The sunlight was shining now between

the curtains which were blowing in the breeze from the open window. She did not speak and the knock came again.

She realised what she must look like on her bed in her embroidered evening gown. There was nothing she could do about it.

"Come in!" she said.

The door opened and she saw, to her relief, it was only Annette who stood there.

"*Ma'm'selle* is wanted . . ." she began in French, only to exclaim: "*Tiens! Ma'm'selle* is still wearing her beautiful gown!"

Varia raised herself slowly.

"I think . . . I fell asleep," she said a little lamely.

"It is creased, but I will iron it," Annette said. Then added hastily: "I had forgotten. *Ma'm'selle* is wanted on the telephone."

"No, no, I will not speak," Varia said quickly, thinking that it must be Pierre who was ringing her.

"It is a call from Switzerland," Annette said.

"Switzerland! It must be my mother."

Annette crossed the room.

"If *Ma'm'selle* will just slip off her dress . . ." she suggested. "It is Henri who has taken the call and sent me to waken you. He will think it is a little strange if *Ma'm'selle* is still wearing that beautiful gown."

"Yes, yes, of course," Varia said.

She let Annette undo the back of the dress, let it fall to the floor and stepped out of it.

Then she quickly slipped into a pretty satin dressing-gown and hurried downstairs and into the little room off the hall where she saw Henri waiting by the telephone.

He had the receiver to his ear and looked up as she appeared.

"Ma'm'selle est ici," the manservant said to the operator. "It is a personal call from Switzerland, *Ma'm'selle,*" he added to Varia.

Varia took the receiver from him and then a man's voice said in English, with only a very slight accent:

"Is that Miss Milfield speaking?"

"Yes, I am Varia Milfield," Varia replied.

"This is Dr. Berger."

"Oh, Dr. Berger!" Varia exclaimed, remembering that he was the head of the Sanatorium where her mother was staying. "How is my mother? Is there anything wrong?"

"I am afraid, Miss Milfield, you must be prepared for rather bad news," the doctor said. "Your mother has taken a turn for the worse. I should like you to come to Lausanne as quickly as possible."

"She's not . . . dead?" Varia asked, hardly able to say the words but forcing them to her lips.

"No, Miss Milfield, your mother is alive," was the reply, "but her condition is very grave. I think it only right that I should tell you the truth."

"Yes, of course, I would much rather know," Varia told him.

"Then will you make every effort to get here as quickly as possible? There is sure to be a plane some time this morning."

"I will be on it," Varia told him.

"Thank you, Miss Milfield."

She heard the click and the line went dead. She stood for a moment wondering what she should do and what was the quickest way to do it.

She opened the door of the room. Henri was outside in the hall, polishing the furniture wearing a striped waistcoat and a large blue apron.

"Henri, I have got to leave for Switzerland at once," Varia said. "Where is the airport and how can I find out how soon an aeroplane will be leaving for Lausanne?"

"I will do that for you," Henri said. "You get dressed, *Ma'm'selle*. Ask Annette to help you. As soon as I know what time the aeroplane is leaving, I will

184

come and knock on your door."

"Thank you, Henri," Varia said gratefully.

She hurried up the stairs and then, as she reached the landing, she thought of Ian. She must tell him and she could also ask him to drive her to the airport.

After a moment's indecision she walked to his door and knocked on it gently. There was no response and, afraid of waking the Duflots, she turned the handle and looked inside.

The curtains were pulled back from the window, the sunlight was streaming in, but there was no-one in the room and the bed had not been slept in. She stared for a moment, half believing that he must be somewhere in the room.

Then she shut the door and hurried away down the corridor.

Annette was hanging up her dress as she came in through the doorway.

"Henri is going to let us know what time an aeroplane is leaving for Lausanne," she said. "Please pack just a few things — anything that I am likely to want."

"It is bad news, *Ma'm'selle?*" Annette asked sympathetically.

"My mother," Varia said briefly.

Somehow she felt she couldn't talk about

185

it, even to someone as sympathetic as Arnette. She had not fully realised yet the full impact of the doctor's words.

She was only conscious of a kind of heavy weight sitting on her heart, a feeling that was a physical pain, making it difficult for her even to think of her mother, let alone mention her.

Somehow nothing mattered beside the fact that her mother was dying. Pierre, Ian, and anybody she had ever known became shadowy figures and of little consequence.

Automatically she slipped into the dress that Annette chose for her. There was a knock on the door and she rushed across the room to open it.

"There is an aeroplane at eight o'clock, *Ma'm'selle,*" Henri said. "You are fortunate, for there is one seat left. I have engaged it for you."

"Thank you, Henri. Thank you very much!" Varia exclaimed. "I would like a taxi please. Can you get me one?"

Henri nodded and glanced down the stairs behind him at the clock ticking in the corner of the hall.

"You should leave about seven," he said. "That will give you a quarter-of-an-hour for some breakfast and for Annette to finish your packing."

Varia did not feel like eating, but to please Henri she forced down half a cup of coffee and nibbled at the fresh *brioche* he brought her. Her throat felt dry and full and it was almost impossible to swallow it.

It was with relief that she heard him announce the taxi had arrived.

"Please tell Madame Duflot how sorry I am to go away like this," she said to Annette. "Explain that my mother is very ill and thank her for all her kindness."

"You will be coming back, *Ma'm'selle?*" Annette said. "And if you do not, what shall I do with your clothes?"

"Pack them up and give them to Mr. Blakewell," Varia answered.

"Oui, oui," Annette answered.

On an impulse Varia bent and kissed the French girl's cheek.

"Thank you for all your kindness, Annette," she said. "And because you have been so kind, would you like to have the dress I was wearing last night? Perhaps you could wear it when you go to a Ball."

It was an impulsive, rather ridiculous gesture on Varia's part, but Annette's face lit up with excitement.

"Do you really mean that, *Ma'm'selle?*" she asked. "I would love that dress more than any dress I have ever seen. I will make sleeves, fill in the *décolletage* a little and then I can be married in it. It will be a wedding dress more beautiful than any girl in my village has ever dreamed of — let alone seen."

"Then it is yours, Annette," Varia said.

Just for a moment the question came to her mind as to what Sir Edward might say abut it. She expected that all the models from Mr. Myles would have to go back into stock when she had finished with them.

Well, this dress would be missing, and she for one could never bear to see it again, not even for the ceremony of handing it back to Madame René.

With something suspiciously like a sob she turned away from Annette and hurried down the stairs, Henri following her with her suitcase.

The taxi was outside the door. She got into it.

For one moment she wondered where Ian was and what he would say when he found her gone.

'What does it matter what he thinks?' she asked herself wearily.

He would be glad to be rid of her. In fact, after what had happened last night it would have been hard to meet him again and have to pretend in front of the Duflots that all was well between them.

Her thoughts were centred on her mother as she travelled to the airport, bought her ticket and joined the queue for the plane.

The fare to Lausanne used up a lot of her money, but there was a little left, and when finally she was in the plane and it was setting off down the runway she had a sudden longing for someone she knew beside her.

She remembered all too vividly the clasp of Ian's hand as they set off from London Airport.

It was the first time, she thought, that he had ever been kind to her. The first time he had not looked at her with hostility and hatred.

The plane turned to take off and suddenly the fear that they would crash gripped her like a vice. Oh, if only Ian were there to tell her not to be afraid.

And then almost as if it was happening, she could feel the touch of his lips on hers, that gentle kiss.

A kiss that had seemed so utterly and completely different from any kiss that she had ever known before.

Ian's mouth holding her captive, and yet so gently that it brought a strange peace both to her heart and mind.

She opened her eyes.

They were up in the air and she had not even realised that they had left the ground.

Yet, astonishingly, she was no longer afraid — and it was the memory of Ian's lips that had taken her fear from her.

Varia sat looking over Lake Geneva.

The water, the sky, the islands, the mountains in the distance, were all blue. It was breathtakingly beautiful, but Varia saw none of it.

She was deep in a world of her own darkness, a world lonely and empty in which she had no-one to turn to, no-one to whom she belonged.

After the funeral — simple, and in its very simplicity a lovely ceremony — was over, Dr. Berger had said to her:

"Go into the garden. I know you want to be alone."

She had not answered him, but turned blindly away from the long, white buildings of the Sanatorium to where the garden with its brilliant flowers, scented shrubs and sheltering trees grew luxuriantly down the hill-side, making a perfect paradise of peace and rest.

She walked until she was out of sight of any building, then sat down on a little wooden seat, where the only sound was the buzz of bees and the chirp of the crickets.

She moved automatically, almost as if someone other than herself directed her legs.

Now she was very still, conscious only of the darkness within her soul, a misery and unhappiness that was past tears.

It seemed to her that ever since she arrived from Lyons in the aeroplane and stepped out on to the airport at Lausanne, she had entered a tunnel of desolation from which there was no escape.

It had been almost a nightmare to hear Dr. Berger's quiet voice telling her what she already knew in her heart.

"I'm afraid, Miss Milfield," he had said, "that you must face the truth. Your mother cannot live much longer. A few hours — perhaps for the rest of the day — that is all the hope I can give you. She has, in fact, hung on to life because she wished to see you."

He paused, his eyes behind the tinted spectacles very gentle.

"There is only one thing I can say to cheer you up. She is in no pain. We have been able to prevent her suffering as she would have suffered if she had not come to us. But we cannot perform miracles, and your mother is past our help."

"Why? Why should this have to happen?" Varia asked impetuously.

"That is what we always ask ourselves when we meet death," Dr. Berger said gravely. "I can say this in all sincerity, she is not afraid to die. In fact, she almost seems to welcome it."

"That, I think, is because she believes that she will be with my father," Varia said. "We have talked of these things very often together, and she has always told me that except for me she would have wanted to die the very day that he did."

The Doctor nodded.

"Was your father's name John?" he asked.

"Yes," Varia replied.

"I thought so," the Doctor nodded. "Your mother has called that name out often in her sleep."

Dr. Berger led Varia into the small but prettily furnished room which had big windows looking out over the flower-filled garden and beyond the garden to the lake.

The sun awnings above the windows were down and it was cool and peaceful.

Varia could see her mother lying very still in the high hospital bed, her face strangely small and pale against the spotless white of the pillows.

With a tremendous effort she forced a

smile to her lips as she approached her side and with her warm fingers covered the cold, emaciated hand which lay outside the bedclothes.

"Mummy, I'm here!" she said, and with difficulty prevented her voice from breaking on the words.

It seemed to her as if her mother's mind came back from a long, long distance.

"Varia?" she exclaimed softly.

"I am here, Mummy!" Varia repeated. "Oh, darling Mummy, I am here with you."

"I wanted . . . to see . . . you," Mrs. Milfield murmured hardly above her breath.

Varia knelt down beside the bed so that her head was on a level with her mother's lips.

There was an inexpressible comfort in being close to her, in knowing that they were together even in this strange room in a land of strangers.

"I . . . want . . . to tell . . . you something." Mrs. Milfield's voice was a little stronger.

"Tell me then," Varia begged.

"I am . . . going to . . . die," her mother said. "I . . . know that . . . but you are . . . not to . . . mind . . . not to . . . be unhappy."

"Oh, Mummy, how could I help it?" Varia cried.

"You are . . . young," Mrs. Milfield answered. "There is . . . so much for . . . you to . . . do. I have . . . tried to . . . look after you . . . but . . . I can do so . . . no longer. I am . . . going to . . . join . . . John."

"Yes, darling, but I shall be lost without you. Oh, Mummy! How can I manage if you are not there?"

A very faint smile touched Mrs. Milfield's lips.

"You will . . . be happy . . . darling," she said very softly. "Very happy . . . I like him . . . very much."

Varia stared at her mother in astonishment. What did she mean? Whom was she talking about? As the questions trembled on her lips, they were arrested by a look of ecstasy which suddenly transformed her mother's face.

For one moment it seemed to Varia as if the lines vanished, the years slipped away and her mother was no longer old, ill and emaciated by suffering, but young and lovely and vital as she had been in her youth.

Her eyes opened wide and then her voice, suddenly clear and strong, rang out across the room.

"Oh, John! John!" she exclaimed.

She made an effort as if to hold out her arms; just for a moment they were raised in the air before they fell back, limp and life-less, against the counterpane.

Varia knew in that second that her mother had gone.

There was something, somebody left in the bed, but it was not her mother.

Young and lovely again, she was joined indivisibly and forever with her husband who had come to fetch her.

Varia knew all this even though, for the moment, she could not put it into words, could only kneel silently and without tears beside the bed until someone helped her to her feet and took her away into another room.

Now, sitting on the wooden seat in the garden, she saw herself travelling back to London alone; felt the emptiness of the little flat in the Mews; saw herself trying to find another job, coming back at night to cook her own meal, to sit in silence, reading or thinking, until she went to bed.

She saw the years stretching ahead with nothing else in them but that, and she felt herself shrink in terror from the idea of it.

She had not spoken to Ian although she knew he had telephoned almost daily.

With what was a note of panic in her voice, she had told Dr. Berger that she could not speak to him, neither could she see anyone.

She had been eternally grateful because the Doctor had not argued.

'I suppose I must leave for England to-morrow,' Varia told herself.

She felt suddenly limp at the thought of arranging her journey, of getting her tickets, of deciding whether she should travel by air or train.

It was then, as she thought of this, that she became conscious of footsteps approaching from behind her.

She turned her head and then started to her feet with a little exclamation of sheer horror.

It was Pierre who stood there. Pierre, dark and handsome; the very last person she expected to see at such a moment.

"Don't be afraid," he said. "Please, Varia, don't be afraid of me."

His tone was almost humble and she realised, with a sense of surprise, that he was smiling at her, not with the flashing, conquering smile with which she was so familiar, but deprecatingly and rather apologetically.

"What do you . . . want?" she asked, and her voice was breathless because she was so astonished to see him.

"I have come to apologise," he said. "You mustn't be angry with Dr. Berger for letting me in. I have been telephoning every day since you got here, begging him to allow me to see you."

"I . . . didn't know," Varia said.

Looking at him she saw that there was a long, discoloured bruise on one side of his face and that there was a newly healed scar on his lower lip which was also surrounded by the dark blueness of a bruise.

"I am sorry about your mother," Pierre said.

The kindness in his tone made the tears prick Varia's eyes for the first time since her mother had died.

She had not been able to cry, although she had known it would have been easier for her if she could.

"We won't talk of it," Pierre said quickly. "But I wanted you to know I was sorry. I came here to say how sorry I was, too, about the way I behaved the other night."

Varia felt herself shiver and try to avoid thoughts of what had happened in the château.

"I know that what I did was unforgivable," Pierre said. "But, in a way, it was your fault."

"My fault?" Varia asked the question in surprise.

"Yes, your fault," he repeated gravely.

"You see, I had only found out that evening about you and Blakewell. I suppose it had been in the papers before, but I had not seen it. I thought you were different from other women. I thought you were transparently frank and innocent and above all the tricks and subterfuges with which so many women muddle their lives."

Raising his eyes, he looked at her averted head as he added:

"I think the knowledge that you had not told me about your engagement, that you loved another man enough to marry him, drove me insane; *mon Dieu,* but that was the truth — I loved you!"

He paused for a moment and then went on:

"I know I've got a rotten reputation. *Cherchez la femme!* Women have always been trouble in my life — I think because they have been too easy. Any women to whom I took a fancy always seemed to come, not half way to meet me but the whole way, if it came to that. I am not making excuses. I am only telling you what are true facts."

"You don't have to tell me all this," Varia said feeling embarrassed by his frankness.

"I've got to," Pierre said simply. "I've got to make you understand. You see, I fell in

198

love with you, *de tout mon coeur,* and that was why you were different from all the other women I had thought I loved but who, in reality, had meant nothing to me."

"Please Pierre, it is too late to say all this now," Varia said.

"*Oui je connais,*" he answered sadly. "I know what you feel about me. I saw your face that night, after I had told you that the girl in the photograph was my *fiancée.* I knew then that I had burned my boats, but because I wanted you so desperately I was determined to have you whether you wanted me or not. It was your fault for not telling me about Blakewell."

"It was wrong of me," Varia replied. "Very wrong of me. But it isn't quite what you think. Ian and I don't love each other."

Even as she said the words, she felt as if she was being disloyal. And yet somehow she could not let Pierre think that she had deceived him so deeply.

"Have you never loved him?" she heard him ask.

She shook her head.

"No," she answered. "There are . . . reasons why we became engaged; reasons that I cannot tell you because they concern Ian. Yet because of what you have told me I will tell you something in confidence. Ian and I will . . . never get . . . married."

"Varia!"

Her name was a cry, and Pierre put out his hands towards her.

She shook her head.

"No, Pierre," she answered firmly. "It is too late."

She saw the light die out of his face and hated herself for hurting him. There was nothing else she could do.

He had killed any tenderness she might have had for him when his kisses had bruised her mouth, when she had known that she was powerless to fight against his strength and he would accord her no mercy.

"Please listen to me, Varia," Pierre pleaded. "My engagement is a formality which means absolutely nothing to me personally. It will cause trouble in my family, but I can be free of it tomorrow if you will marry me. I swear to you that I will try to make you happy and that I will love you devotedly until the end of my life."

'He means it,' Varia thought to herself, in all sincerity.

She knew that a fortnight ago she would have believed him. Now, because she was older and wiser and very much more sophisticated, she was well aware that it would be impossible for Pierre to love anybody for very long.

"Thank you, Pierre," she said gently. "But I can never love you. I know that now."

"I could have made you," he said. "If all this had not happened, if we had gone on as we were, I could have made you love me, couldn't I?"

"I don't think so," Varia answered. "I was attracted by you, dazzled by you because you were so unlike anyone else I had ever met in my life before. But in reality we are poles apart, you and I. I want security and peace, and the love of somebody who will never want anyone else but me, and whom I will love until I die."

"I will never love anyone but you," Pierre said quickly. "I could teach you how to love me and you would find it easy because I love you so much."

Varia wrinkled her brow.

"It is funny," she said. "But all the things I felt about you have now gone. And now, I just like you. I can see exactly what you are — the nice things, the nasty things and the really horrible things about you. I am sorry for the latter and I should like to help you, but I couldn't feel anything else except just a liking which I wish could become a real friendship."

He got to his feet and stood looking down at her.

"Je comprends," he said. "I know when I am beaten, but somehow I don't believe that it is all my fault that it is finished. I think, if you ask me, you are half in love with that stuck-up Englishman. Perhaps you will marry him after all."

He bent down and took her hand again.

"Good-bye, Varia," he said. "I will never forget you. You will be the one woman in my life whom I shall always regret having lost. Does that mean anything to you?"

"A great deal," Varia answered. "But it doesn't make me change my mind. Good-bye, Pierre."

"Au revoir, ma petite!" he said. "Thank you for giving me a glimpse of what spring should really be like; for making me know what I have been looking for all my life and what I shall go on looking for. *Je t'adore.*"

He kissed her hand and then, without another word, turned and walked away. She didn't watch him go, but she listened until his footsteps on the garden path died into silence.

She almost had an impulse to call him back.

Why was she so foolish as to send him away? She might not love him, but at least he would have helped her loneliness.

It would have been nice to be with him, fun to listen to his compliments. And then she knew that it was no use. It was all or nothing with Pierre.

She gave a little sigh and turning her back on the loveliness of the lake, walked back towards the Sanatorium.

As she walked in through the garden door, Dr. Berger's secretary came out of the office.

"Oh, there you are, Miss Milfield," she said. "I was just coming to look for you. There is a telephone call for you. The Doctor wasn't certain whether you wished to take it."

"Who is it?" Varia asked, although she already knew the answer.

"It is Mr. Ian Blakewell," the secretary replied. "He rings every day."

"I will speak to him," Varia said.

She went into the small room off the office where patients, seated in comfortable chairs overlooking the garden, could make their private telephone calls.

Varia picked up the receiver and after a moment she heard a click which meant that the secretary had switched through the call.

"Hello!" she said, her voice sounding stiff and restrained even to herself.

"Hello!" it was Ian's voice. "Will Miss Milfield speak to me?"

"It's Varia speaking," she said with an effort.

"Varia; I've been trying to get hold of you for days. The Doctor said you wouldn't take any calls."

"No, I didn't feel like it."

There was a moment's pause and then Ian said:

"I am terribly sorry, you know that, don't you?"

"Yes, of course. Thank you."

It was then that something came to Varia's mind for the first time since that night at the château. She had forgotten completely the reason why she had gone to the château and what Pierre had told her.

With a little gasp she said:

"Ian, I have something to tell you, something very important."

"I'd better come along then, right away," he said.

"Right away? What do you mean?"

"I'm in Lausanne," he answered. "At an hotel."

"Oh, I had no idea!"

"I got here the day before yesterday. Shall I come to you now, this moment, or would you rather I waited?"

204

His question made Varia hesitate, why she did not know.

"Perhaps . . ." she began, and then forced herself to take the plunge. "Now! Come now!"

"Very well. It will take about ten minutes."

She heard Ian put down the receiver and then, very slowly, she replaced her own.

Why, she wondered, did she feel so reluctant to see him? Why had it made her feel almost frightened to know that he was here in Lausanne?

She opened the door and walked back into the garden, down the path and towards the wooden seat on which she had been sitting when Pierre found her.

Ian would be sent there, she was certain of that. And somehow she felt it would be easier to meet him in the open than in a room where it would be hard to avoid looking at each other.

It would be so much easier not to have to face Ian again, remembering what she was trying to forget — that last moment she had been with him and he had kissed her in the darkness of the passage!

She heard him coming down the path. Because she was shy and nervous she rose to her feet and stood facing him, on the defensive, her eyes wary, like a fawn that has been startled in the undergrowth.

"I say, isn't it lovely here?" Ian exclaimed, looking at the lake below them. "I always think Lausanne is one of the prettiest places in the world."

"I haven't seen many, so I'm not able to judge," Varia answered. "But I don't believe any place could be more lovely."

"You ought to see Venice," he said. "I think you would enjoy that."

"I don't think there's much chance of my seeing Venice, or anywhere else except London," Varia answered. "I suppose you've come to tell me that I must go back."

"I didn't know what you wanted to do," he replied.

"But of course, I must go back," Varia answered almost sharply. "I was thinking of asking Dr. Berger to arrange it."

"I'll do that," Ian said simply. "There's a plane about noon tomorrow if that would suit you."

"Yes of course," Varia said.

He looked out over the lake, and then, almost as if the words were rather difficult, he said:

"Is there anything I can do to help?"

Varia knew exactly to what he referred.

"No, nothing," she answered. "I am not

unhappy for my mother, only for myself. You see, I shall miss her so much."

Ian was very still for a moment and then he said:

"I missed my mother when she died. That is why I have always tried to look after my father and to do what he wanted. I think she would have liked it."

"I can't imagine you being lonely somehow," Varia said.

"Nevertheless I am very lonely at times," Ian said with a little smile.

"Perhaps that's why you went out with . . ."

Varia stopped suddenly. She had been going to say "with people like Lareen," and then she thought it was rude.

"Listen Ian! I have got something to tell you," she said quickly. "Something I ought to have told you before, but I forgot about it. It's something . . . Pierre told me."

She felt Ian stiffen, and went on quickly, not looking at him:

"You never asked me for an explanation as to why I went to Pierre's house that evening. The truth is that he told me he could tell me something about Lareen — something which I felt might be of help to you. He wouldn't tell me what it was unless . . . unless I promised to see his château."

"Just the sort of bargain the swine would

drive," Ian muttered almost beneath his breath.

"I don't want to talk about what happened," Varia said hastily. "I just want to tell you what Pierre told me. He said that Lareen is married to the son of the overseer on his father's estate in Morocco. She's never had a divorce although they parted several years ago."

"Lareen married! Good Lord!" Ian ejaculated. "That's the last thing I should have expected."

"Pierre was quite certain it was true," Varia insisted. "I think if you tackle her with it she would not be inclined to bring a breach of promise case against you, which could only result in raking up scandals for herself."

"I'm quite certain she won't," Ian said. "As a matter of fact, I never believed Lareen's threats. She always gets very hysterical and abusive when she's cross, but usually her tantrums are forgotten as soon as she's in a good temper again."

Varia felt deflated, as if her information, which she had expected to be so sensational, missed fire.

"I just thought you would be interested in what I had heard," she said a little stiffly.

"I am, of course," Ian answered. "And

thank you for finding it out for me."

He hesitated, then added:

"Did you really go to de Chalayat's house just because you felt it would be of help to me?"

"Yes, I promise you that's the truth," Varia answered.

"But why? Why did you do that when you hate me so much?" Ian enquired.

"I, hate you?"

Varia sounded surprised.

"Yes, of course," he replied. "You've shown it pretty obviously ever since we came on this trip."

"But that's ridiculous!" Varia exclaimed, half laughing. "You hated me. Look at the way you fought against your father asking me to take the job at all. I saw the way you looked at me. If there was any hating to be done, you were doing it."

"Well, it's hardly surprising," Ian said hotly. "After all, nobody wants to be forced into an engagement with someone who's obviously been bribed to undertake the job and who dislikes the very thought of it. Besides, I saw at once it was only a trick of my father's to get me free of Lareen and into the right sort of mind to accept another of his propositions — marriage with a girl he had already picked out as being highly desirable for me."

"You mean he wants you to get married?" Varia asked.

"Yes, of course," Ian answered. "You don't know the old man. His one idea in life is to push people about like pawns on a chess-board. Oh, he had it all tied up nicely. My engagement to you was to finish my entanglements with Lareen once and for all, besides, of course, settling any aspirations the Duflots might have in my direction."

He gave a little laugh with no humour in it.

"This makes me sound like a conceited fool, but when we get back you will find he's got another plan all ready. You will be thanked for your services and paid off, and I shall be led like a sheep to the slaughter and married off to this society girl he's got lined up."

There was so much bitterness and suffused anger in Ian's face that Varia could not help throwing back her head and laughing.

"Oh, it's too ridiculous!" she exclaimed, "and I don't believe a word of it."

Ian shrugged his shoulders.

"Very well," he said. "But you will soon see that's the truth!"

"But you — what are you going to say

about it all?" Varia asked. "Surely you've got a will of your own. Do you know this girl? Do you like her?"

She was conscious, as she spoke, of a sudden overwhelming curiosity, and of some other feeling she could not quite analyse.

"I will tell you one thing," Ian said slowly, "I am going to do one of the things that my father wants — I am going to ask the girl with whom I have fallen in love to marry me."

Varia did not know why, but it seemed to her suddenly as if the sun had gone in.

It was cold and she felt herself shiver as she answered, in a hesitant and curiously flat voice.

"I . . . do hope you will be . . . very happy."

Chapter Six

"You are going back . . . back . . . back!"

The noise of the engines seemed to repeat the words over and over again until Varia thought that everyone in the aeroplane must hear them.

Back to London! Back to loneliness.

Back to an aching emptiness because her mother would not be there.

"You are not frightened, are you?" Ian asked. "You are getting quite a seasoned traveller."

"I suppose I am," she answered dully, feeling that this was perhaps the last journey she would ever take.

She was never likely to have the money to come abroad again. And she couldn't expect to get a job which was anything more than routine office work in some noisy London street.

"What are you going to do when you get back?" he asked, as if in some unexpected, intuitive way he sensed her thoughts.

"I haven't decided yet," she replied.

"You wouldn't want to go back to Blakewell and Company?" he asked.

"It would be rather awkward, wouldn't it?" she retorted, not looking at him. "Think what they must be saying in the office now about our . . . our engagement. And when it is broken off they are certain to say you have jilted me. They couldn't imagine my refusing to marry a rich young man like — you."

She couldn't help the sting in her voice and she felt, though she did not look at him, that he winced slightly.

"I have often wondered what the girls in an office think about their employers. Do they hate us so very much?"

"Hate you!" Varia ejaculated. "No, of course not. But you do seem rather aloof and out of touch. I think the fact is that we look on you as necessary evils."

She laughed at her own joke but Ian did not smile.

"A necessary evil!" he said. "Not a very enviable thing to be."

"You mustn't judge by me," Varia said quickly. "I expect really most of the girls admire you, even if they pretend they don't. I know that sometimes they would come and say they had met you on the stairs, and be quite coy about it."

"And you never felt like that?" Ian enquired.

Varia shook her head.

"I don't think I have ever learned how to be coy," she said with a smile. "And besides, I had only seen you once or twice before your father called me into the office."

"Then what did you think?"

He seemed rather anxious to know her opinion and for a moment she hesitated, looking back at her feelings and emotions when Sir Edward had put that strange, unexpected proposition to her.

"I think," she said at length slowly, "I was sorry for you because you obviously hated so much the idea of our pretended engagement."

"Sorry for me!" Ian ejaculated.

It was obviously a new idea to him and it seemed to Varia as if he digested it quietly to himself.

'Have I been unkind?' she wondered.

She thought that perhaps he was far more vulnerable and easily hurt than she had anticipated. She found herself wondering what the girl was like with whom he was in love.

They would be very happy, she thought,

because Ian was the type of man to make a really good husband.

Thinking suddenly of the gentleness of his kiss that night in the passage, Varia knew that he could also be a very alluring lover, if not such a flamboyant one as Pierre.

She was suddenly conscious that she was knitting her fingers together so tightly that the knuckles showed white. She knew, too, that she was holding herself stiff and tense as if she braced herself against a blow.

And she knew the answer.

She was afraid of her own feelings; afraid of acknowledging, even to herself, the sudden pain within her heart; the dark depression which was even more intense than what had been there before when she was merely feeling lonely.

'Don't be absurd,' she whispered to herself. 'You don't feel like this about him — you can't.'

Yet it was there — a sudden longing; a strange, unaccountable yearning; a violent curiosity about this other girl whom he loved, which amounted, if she dared to face it, to something that was curiously akin to jealousy.

"It isn't true! It isn't true!" she whispered.

She started as Ian asked:

"Did you say anything?"

"No," she answered.

As she said it she looked up and met his eyes — dark grey eyes with unfathomable depths in them.

She knew then, even while she had known it before; knew, by the sudden quickened beating of her heart, by a feeling so intense that as it swept over her she thought that it brought with it almost a sense of fairness.

She put her head back against the chair and shut her eyes.

How could she have been so stupid, so ridiculous, so utterly absurd as to let herself fall in love? For that was the truth and she had to acknowledge it.

She was in love with Ian — had been in love with him for quite some time.

It was because she was attracted to him that she had been so perturbed when she thought he hated her. It was because she had wanted his solid protection that she had winced away from Pierre's ephemeral love-making.

Fool that she was! And yet she should have known the truth when he kissed her and she had felt her own lips respond to the gentleness of his.

She opened her eyes and looked at the golden sunshine above the soft whiteness of the clouds.

'I shall always remember this,' she thought. 'I shall always remember it was now, at this moment, that I knew that I loved him — when it is too late, much, much too late to do anything about it. If I had known sooner, I might have tried to attract him, to make him love me.'

Yet she thought that would have been impossible in the position they both found themselves.

She saw Sir Edward like an evil genie directing their lives, bringing them together and separating them again. He had achieved what he wanted.

He had brought off his commercial coup without difficulty and without any incidents which might affect his future relationship with the Duflots.

There was only one casualty, and that, Varia thought wrily, was her own heart.

Slowly her mind went back over the times they had spent together since that first day when they had met in Sir Edward's office.

She could remember everything, every word that had been said, every gesture that Ian had made.

She could feel his hand on hers when he had realised that she was frightened in the aeroplane, could see him smiling at her when she had come downstairs for the Ball.

She had felt numb when he had said:

"I am going to ask the girl I love to marry me."

Now, when she thought of the words, they had the power to stab her with a hundred little knives of pain and regret.

And yet she had very little, in fact, to regret. She could not have done more. She might perhaps have invited his kisses — and yet, in that case, would he have given them to her?

One would have to be enough to carry her though her life. One kiss, the touch of his hand, the knowledge that they had been together on an exciting adventure which now had come to an end.

"We shall be going down in a moment," Ian's voice broke in on her thoughts.

"So soon?" she asked.

"I thought it seemed rather a long journey," he said.

She told herself that of course he was in a hurry to get home.

She groped for her safety belt, but he fastened it for her.

Then, as she said "Thank you," he held out his hand, palm upwards.

"Quite sure you are not frightened?" he asked with a little smile that was somehow unlike him.

She hesitated for a moment and then,

almost like a diver plunging into a deep, green pool, she gave a little laugh and put her hand into his.

His fingers, warm and strong, closed over hers.

"So you are not so sophisticated as you look," he teased.

"At least I'm glad I look wise!" she answered, trying to speak lightly. "If I do."

"But of course you do," he answered. "Doesn't your looking-glass tell you how much you have altered since we first met? But I'm not certain I didn't prefer you as you were."

"Untidy and dowdy?" she questioned.

"Young and unspoilt," he corrected. "When you came into the office that morning when my father first sent for you, I thought I had never seen anyone so young and so — fresh."

"As a matter of fact I felt very frightened," Varia admitted.

"I know you did," he answered. "And that's what made me so angry."

"Angry?" she enquired.

"That my father should mix you up in his Machiavellian schemes," Ian explained.

Varia tried to follow his conversation, but all she could think of was the fact that Ian was holding her hand.

If she had not known that she was in love with him, she would have known now. Known it because she could feel strange ripples like little magnetic waves running over her whole body.

'So this is what is means to be thrilled,' she thought.

She wondered what he would say if she asked him to kiss her once more — to kiss her good-bye.

She felt herself tremble at the thought. Instantly his voice, felicitous and kind, said:

"You are nervous. You're trembling. I promise you it will be all right."

"I'm not really afraid," Varia tried to say.

She prayed he would never guess that she could not help her fingers quivering because he was touching her.

'I love him! I love him!' she thought to herself, and knew with a little feeling of utter dismay that the aeroplane had touched down.

They were back on British soil. This was the end of the chapter.

She had counted on having a few more moments alone with Ian in the car, but she was to be disappointed. Sir Edward's secretary — a rather talkative middle-aged man with horn-rimmed spectacles — met them and asked innumerable boring and conventional questions about the journey.

He then settled down to talk about the contract that had been arranged with Monsieur Duflot.

Varia sat in silence as they drove back to London.

She was vividly conscious of Ian beside her, his shoulder against hers. She tried not to look at him, instead she looked out on the sunlit countryside and felt that to echo her own mood it should be raining.

"Is my father at the office, Jenkins?" she heard Ian ask.

"No, not today; Sir Edward asked me to say that he hoped both you and Miss Milfield would go straight to Regent's Park," the secretary replied.

"Does that suit you, Varia, or would you rather go home first?" Ian enquired.

"I don't mind," Varia said.

She thought that in a way this was a respite so that she could see him for just a little longer.

She felt the tears start into her eyes.

With an effort she admonished herself to be more sensible. What was the point of yearning after someone she could never have? What was the point of longing for the impossible?

Yet she could not help longing.

'If only I could work for him,' she thought humbly. 'If only I could go back to the office and at least see him occasionally on the stairs or in the lift.'

That in itself would be something.

Mr. Jenkins was chattering again and now they were moving through the traffic in Baker Street towards the house in Regent's Park.

They turned in at the drive and Varia drew a deep breath. This really was the beginning of the end!

She stepped out. The old grey-haired butler led them through the high, marble-floored Hall to the big sitting-room where Varia had come once before and where Ian had put the engagement ring on her finger. She pulled it off now and held it in her hand.

She felt suddenly that her finger would feel empty without the weight of the stone and the encircling band. She would miss its sparkle as she put out her hand.

Although at first she had hated it, she knew it had gradually become something which joined her to Ian.

Sir Edward was sitting in his usual chair, a light rug over his knees. He looked better, Varia thought. His face was not so pale and transparent as it had been the last time she saw him.

"Ah! Ian, my boy!" he exclaimed as they were announced. "Here you are. Only a few minutes late. I had only just begun to worry in case you had missed the plane."

"No, Father. Everything ran according to schedule," Ian said drily.

He shook Sir Edward by the hand, then turned as he did so to include Varia.

"I have brought Varia back safely."

Sir Edward held out his hand.

"I'm glad to see you, my dear," he said. "I was very distressed, though, at the sad news. I am only thankful your mother did not suffer."

"No, they did everything at the Sanatorium that could be done for her," Varia said quietly.

"It is distressing, very distressing for you," Sir Edward said. "Now you must both sit down and tell me all about the trip. It was successful?"

He addressed the last question to Ian.

"Very successful, Father. The contract was agreed in almost the exact terms that you, yourself, desired. In fact, with a very minor alteration, it was almost word for word as you dictated it."

"Good! Very good indeed!" Sir Edward exclaimed. "That was what I hoped to hear."

He turned to Varia.

"And now, my dear, you must tell me what you thought of France. Did you enjoy your first visit?"

"Very much, thank you," Varia answered.

"Varia was a great success," Ian said, and she felt herself flush at the complimentary tone of his voice. "And incidentally, Father, her clothes were the admiration and envy of every woman in Lyons."

"I thought they would be," Sir Edward said. "And now let me say again how grateful I am to you, my dear."

Varia rose to her feet and going towards him held out the ring she had taken from her finger.

"I must give this back to you," she said in a rather flat voice. "And will you tell me what you want done with the clothes that I have been wearing?"

"You must keep them, of course," Ian said quickly before his father could answer.

Sir Edward pursed his lips.

"Well, I don't know about . . . er . . . all of them . . ." he began.

Varia knew as she had suspected already, that he intended the models to be returned to Martin Myles's collection.

"I think," Ian said firmly, "that Varia is entitled to those clothes. All of them."

The eyes of father and son met, and to Varia's astonishment Sir Edward capitulated.

"Of course, if you put it like that, my dear boy," he said, "there is nothing more to be said. I hope, Varia, you will accept the clothes as a present from the firm of Blakewell and Company."

"No, I don't want to take . . ." Varia began, only to be silenced by an almost imperious wave of Ian's hand.

"There are other things to discuss, Father," he said. "First of all, why did you tell the Press of our engagement? They caught up with us just before we boarded the aeroplane at London Airport. Varia and I understood from you that our engagement would be a complete secret except so far as the Duflots were concerned."

Sir Edward looked a little taken aback.

"These things leak out," he said hastily. "When the Press approached me I thought it would be a mistake to lie. One never knows what might appear in the French papers in consequence."

"Not a very good explanation," Ian said coldly. "And secondly, now that I have brought off this particular contract that you wanted so much, I wish to hand in my resignation. I no longer wish to be associated with Blakewell and Company."

His words were spoken in a quiet, even tone, but to Varia, as to Sir Edward, they were sensational.

Both stared at Ian as if he had taken leave of his senses, but he met his father's eyes squarely. Varia had the impression that he was a man who had just laid down a tremendous burden.

"What the devil do you mean?" Sir Edward managed to ejaculate.

"Exactly what I say, Father," Ian replied. "I have not been happy in the firm for some time. I have done what you wished simply and solely because I felt it my duty. Now that, due in a small part to my efforts, Blakewell and Company have a contract which will put them streets ahead of all their competitors, I feel I am free."

"And what, may I ask, do you mean by free?" Sir Edward asked in an ominous tone, his eyes dark with anger.

"I want to go to Canada," Ian said. "As you know, I have always really been interested in engineering. I have the opportunity of joining an engineering company in Toronto. It belongs to a friend of mine who has offered me a partnership. It entails a few years' work in Canada and then the prospect of travelling all over the world. I intend to accept it."

"You intend! You have made up your mind! Who are you to tell me what you are going to do?" Sir Edward thundered, bringing his fist down with a crash on the side of his chair.

He threw the rug off his knees and got to his feet. He moved with agility, with an almost wiry kind of strength which made Varia realise suddenly that he was by no means as frail as he appeared.

Was it a pose, she wondered, which let him give an impression of ill health so that he could get his own way more easily?

Then her thoughts about Sir Edward merged into a sudden realisation that Ian was lost to her for ever.

He was going away, leaving the country. And now, not only figuratively but in actual fact, there would never be the slightest chance of seeing him again.

Like a clap of thunder in her ears she heard Sir Edward shout.

"You'll stay here with me! You'll do as you're told, damn you! You're still my son, and as long as I live there'll be no freedom for you!"

Ian, too, rose to his feet.

"I'm sorry, Father," he said, "but I have been a slave and a fool long enough. I've got to learn not only to work for myself, but to think for myself. I want to make this quite clear now, and we'll talk about it later this evening."

"To hell with this evening! We'll discuss it now," Sir Edward roared.

But Ian shook his head.

"I am going to take Varia home," he said. "She's had a long journey and it is not particularly pleasant for her to hear us quarrelling. I will see you later this evening, Father. In the meantime, here is the contract, and here with it is my resignation from the Company, in writing."

He put the two papers down on the table and Sir Edward stood looking at them with rage and incredulity chasing each other across his features.

Ian turned to Varia.

"Will you come now?" he said.

She rose to her feet and after a quick look at Sir Edward, decided to say nothing but walked towards the door.

Ian opened it for her and they went out through the Hall to where the car was waiting outside the front door.

Varia got into it; Ian sat beside her and the car started off immediately, the chauffeur obviously having already had his instructions where to go.

After a moment or two Varia said:

"Are you really going to Canada?"

"I am leaving in four days' time," Ian said. "I made up my mind a long time ago that I had to break away. My father is a dictator. So long as I remain with him I shall be nothing but a cipher, a mere mouthpiece through which I voice his thoughts."

Varia said nothing, and after a moment he went on:

"It will be an adventure — Canada I mean. I have got to start almost from scratch because my friend hasn't built up his business as yet to anything very big. But we have ideas, we have enthusiasm, and neither of us is afraid of hard work."

"It sounds very exciting," Varia said wistfully.

There seemed nothing else to say and as they travelled swiftly through the traffic she found herself thinking only of the happiness of being near him.

She looked at his hand lying loosely on the seat beside her, and wondered what he would say if she slipped her own into it.

Because she was afraid of herself, she turned her head away to watch the streets flashing by until they turned into the mews and stopped outside her own door.

She fumbled in her bag and found the key

where she had placed it when she left — it seemed to her now a century ago.

Ian followed her up the narrow stairs.

The chauffeur carried in her suitcases and placed them on the small landing at the top. Varia went into the sitting-room. It seemed smaller than she last remembered it.

It was looking rather dusty and strangely empty.

She opened the window and the breeze blew in, making the dust rise a little. Then she turned towards Ian to say good-bye.

He stood in the doorway watching her, and then, to her surprise, he shut the door behind him and came a little further into the room.

The words of politeness and thanks which hovered on her lips died away. He looked at her in what seemed to her a very strange manner, and when her eyes met his she felt suddenly shy and embarrassed.

Because he did not speak she felt she must say something.

"I . . . I want to say . . . thank you . . ." she began, stammering a little in her shyness.

"Are you coming with me?" he asked.

For a moment she did not understand the question, only looking up at him, her eyes very wide.

"What . . . do you mean?" she managed to gasp.

The words that came between her lips were hardly more than a whisper.

"Won't you come?" he asked. "It won't be very luxurious at first, but I know I shall succeed with you to help me."

Still Varia was afraid to guess at his meaning.

Frantically she fought against a sudden warmth which seemed to be pervading her whole body. Frantically, she clutched at her commonsense, at her sanity.

"You mean that you want . . . a secretary?" she faltered.

His grave face broke into a smile.

"Oh, darling!" he said. "Do you really believe I am asking you to be anything so idiotic? You know what I want. I have already told you I wanted to ask the girl I love to be my wife."

"But . . . but that's . . . that's not me," Varia said pathetically.

"Of course it's you," he answered. "Haven't you known all the time? Didn't you know when you drove me nearly mad with jealousy and I wanted to kill the unknown man you were meeting at night? Then, when I discovered it was de Chalayat I was very near to murder. I shall never forget my rage when I saw him kissing you. If any man has had a lucky escape from death it is he."

Varia's hand went to quell the tumult in her breasts.

"Why . . . didn't you . . . tell me?" she asked.

"How could I?" Ian replied. "You were under my protection in very special circumstances. You were with me under a mad, crazy arrangement made by my father. And so I could only love you and say nothing."

He gave a little laugh, then went on:

"I was so angry and so wild that night after I had rescued you from de Chalayat that I did something that I have been longing to do for days — or was it years? I kissed you. And I knew then, as I had never known it before, that you were the only person in the world for me. I love you, Varia! Please come with me to Canada?"

She felt as if she were walking on the soft white clouds tipped with sunshine which they had left behind in the sky.

She felt as if the whole world whirled around her and disappeared and that she was alone with Ian; that there was nobody else and nothing else — there were only the two of them.

For a moment she could not speak, could not move.

She could only stand looking at him, her

eyes held by his, her whole body trembling with the ecstasy that rippled over her.

And then suddenly she was in his arms and he was holding her very close.

"Don't say no," he was begging her in a voice which was suddenly sharpened with fear. "I'm so frightened of losing you, so frightened you won't want me after all we've had to do together."

"But I . . . do," Varia tried to whisper, and yet somehow the words wouldn't come.

She felt it was all too glorious, too wonderful to be borne. There was a constriction in her throat and she was unable to say anything.

As if Ian understood he bent his head with an emotion that was past passion, and laid his cheek against hers.

"My sweet, my darling!" he whispered in her ear. "You are so young and lovely that I'm afraid of you. Please say you love me a little bit, and I will give my whole life to making you love me more."

He moved his head back so that he could look down into her face, and now the wonder of her eyes said all that her lips could not speak. He looked down into them for a long, long moment.

Then his mouth was on hers.

"I love you!" he murmured. "Darling

little Varia, I love you!"

She made a sound that was lost against his lips and felt herself caught up into an ecstasy so glorious and so wonderful that there was no need for words.

This was life, this was adventure, this was love — all in the magic of Ian's kiss.

About the Author

Barbara Cartland, who sadly died in May 2000 at the age of nearly ninety-nine, was the world's most famous romantic novelist. She wrote 723 books in her lifetime, with worldwide sales of over one billion copies and her books were translated into thirty-six different languages.

As well as romantic novels, she wrote historical biographies, six autobiographies, theatrical plays, books of advice on life, love, vitamins and cookery. She also found time to be a political speaker and television and radio personality.

She wrote her first book at the age of twenty-one and this was called *Jigsaw*. It became an immediate bestseller and sold 100,000 copies in hardback and was translated into six different languages. She wrote continuously throughout her life, writing bestsellers for an astonishing seventy-six years. Her books have always been immensely popular in the United States, where in 1976 her current books were at numbers one and two in the B. Dalton bestsellers list, a feat never achieved before or since by any author.

Barbara Cartland became a legend in her own lifetime and will be remembered for her wonderful romantic novels, so loved by her millions of readers throughout the world.

Her books will always be treasured for their moral message, her pure and innocent heroines, her good-looking and dashing heroes and above all her belief that the power of love is more important than anything else in everyone's life.

We hope you have enjoyed this Large Print book. Other Thorndike, Wheeler or Chivers Press Large Print books are available at your library or directly from the publishers.

For more information about current and upcoming titles, please call or write, without obligation, to:

Publisher
Thorndike Press
295 Kennedy Memorial Drive
Waterville, ME   04901
Tel. (800) 223-1244

Or visit our Web site at:
www.thomson.com/thorndike
www.thomson.com/wheeler

OR

Chivers Large Print
published by BBC Audiobooks Ltd
St James House, The Square
Lower Bristol Road
Bath BA2 3BH
England
Tel. +44(0) 800 136919
email: bbcaudiobooks@bbc.co.uk
www.bbcaudiobooks.co.uk

All our Large Print titles are designed for easy reading, and all our books are made to last.